A. N. Wilson is a confirmed ... :ular affection for cats, whom he strongly believes "are as much individuals as you or I." It is a conviction he takes very seriously and, while he does not think he romanticises cats, he says that "I can think of many ways in which I would be a better person if I were more like my cats, but I cannot think of a single way in which my cats would be any better for being more like me."

A distinguished novelist, biographer, critic and Fellow of the Royal Society of Literature, A. N. Wilson has won several prestigious awards – notably, on two occasions, the John Llewellyn Rhys Memorial Prize (for *The Sweets of Pimlico* and *The Laird of Abbotsford*), the 1981 Somerset Maugham Award (for *The Healing Art*) and the 1988 Whitbread Award (for the biography *Tolstoy*).

Stray is his first book about cats – but not his last: "While writing it I was more caught up in the adventure than I have been with any of my previous stories about two-footers," he says, and has now written a picture book about *Tabitha* – as well as a volume of guinea-pig stories called *Hazel* (both published by Walker Books).

Also by A N Wilson

NOVELS

The Sweets of Pimlico
Unguarded Hours
Kindly Light
The Healing Art
Who Was Oswald Fish?
Wise Virgin
Scandal
Gentlemen in England
Love Unknown
Incline Our Hearts

BIOGRAPHIES

The Laird of Abbotsford
A Life of John Milton
Hilaire Belloc
Tolstoy

CHILDREN'S BOOKS

The Tabitha Stories
Hazel the Guinea-Pig

STRAY

A. N. WILSON

WALKER BOOKS
LONDON

"A. N. Wilson has pulled a very distinguished cat out of his hat. It is an excellent book ... I hope you will all buy it, read it and pass it on to your children."
Harriet Waugh, *The Spectator*

"Even a dedicated ornithologist and cat-hater such as myself can find a good deal to enjoy here ... This cat's-eye view of life is engagingly low, with some neat floor-level observations of the human species."
The London Review of Books

"A. N. Wilson was clearly enjoying himself when he wrote *Stray* ... Definitely a cat-lover's book, it creates a convincing feline world ... and the story is always immensely readable."
Nigel Andrew, *The Listener*

"Try it. It makes you realise that two legs good, four legs sometimes better."
She

"This imaginative 'autobiography' of Pufftail, an astringently articulate alley-cat ... certainly justifies its publisher's claim that it is for 'cat lovers of all ages'. Its racy fluency of incident and dialogue should hold youthful interest without difficulty ... The author conveys a powerful and angry sympathy for cats and all they suffer."
Geoffrey Trease, *British Book News*

"An epic story, etched into the imagination by the quality of the writing. Imagine *Black Beauty* written with some of the vitriol of *Watership Down* ... and you come somewhere near translating the extraordinary effect of the novel."
George English, *BBC Radio*

For A.L.R.

**You who have written much of this and that,
Reserved your kindest comments for a cat.**

**First published 1987 by Walker Books Ltd
87 Vauxhall Walk, London SE11 5HJ**

© 1987 A. N. Wilson
Cover illustration by Sarah Fox-Davies

This edition published 1989
Reprinted 1989

Printed in Great Britain by Richard Clay Ltd, Bungay, Suffolk
Typeset in Hong Kong by Graphicraft Typesetters Ltd

British Library Cataloguing in Publication Data
Wilson, A. N.
Stray.
I. Title
823'.914 [F]
ISBN 0-7445-0842-8

CHAPTER ONE

Like all our race I was born blind and it was some days
before I opened my eyes. Even when I could see I did not
make much of what I saw. I suppose that this is partly
because I was so small and the world was so big. I could see
my brothers and my sister, snuggling, as I was, next to our
mother. And I could see my mother – then. Often since I
grew up I have seen a female cat suckling her young and I
have tried to remember my own mother. I know that she
was tabby with white markings – as I am myself – but I
cannot remember her features. I can only remember the
feeling of warmth and security I enjoyed for those first few
days and weeks of my life, when I was alone somewhere, in
a room, with just my mother and my brothers and my sister
and no intrusion from the human world.

My mother must have had decent human minders. They
had let her give birth to us. They had not drowned us as so
many people drown kittens; and, as I say, they left us in
peace. Being born and coming to life was for me like waking
up after a long, delightfully deep and lazy sleep. There was
no hurry about waking up. As I have told you, little grandson, for the first few days I did not even open my eyes. And
then for quite a few days more I simply lay there, squeaking
and purring with my tiny voice, and with a constant supply
of delicious warm milk always laid on by my mother.
Although I cannot remember her appearance, how well I
remember that feeling of well-being, when I was cuddled up
beside her – I think we were in a large open drawer at the
bottom of a bed or a wardrobe – the warmth of her fur, the
tenderness with which she licked us and groomed us and
taught us to be clean.

7

After I was about a fortnight old I became aware that the world was not entirely populated by cats. My mother had begun to tell us that there were *people* in the world. But what could that mean to me when I had no idea what they were like? Then gradually, over the next few days or weeks, my brothers and I got to know the human look and that human smell. The drawer where we were lying peacefully would be roughly shaken and one would hear a grown-up human voice say, "Just peep at them, mind! Don't touch them, yet, or it will disturb them!" or "Aren't they *gorgeous*."

Of course I reconstruct what they said but this is the sort of thing I have heard drooling, well-meaning two-footers say when staring at kittens. And who can blame them? There are no creatures in the world more endearing than young kittens with large eyes and large paws and soft, fluffy little coats. Yes, even I was a young kitten once, though you may find it impossible to believe. Young and frisky and as silly as you. The first thing which struck me about the human beings was not what they said but what they looked like. I remember, when we had been visited a number of times by them, trying to focus my eyes on the enormous red faces which peered so closely at our own. At that stage nothing had happened to make me dread or fear the human race; but I think I did fear them. They seemed so large and, by the refined standards of my own mother, so very coarse and ugly. I remember the extraordinary smells they gave off as they peered at us – you know the human stench already and how horrible it is to animal nostrils.

But, as I say, though I was in the house of human kind, they were reasonably good specimens. Gradually, as we grew older, the people fed us with eggs and boiled chicken until we were used to solid foods. And before long they were feeding us on tinned foods and minced offal, and playing with us. We left the room where we were born and were carried down some stairs in a basket; and there, in front of a big fire, we would scamper about, chase balls of wool, and amuse ourselves and the people in whose house we had been born. They were still happy days, I suppose, but for me the days of pure and true happiness will always be the days in that bedroom, when it was just cats and no human interruptions.

Bright of eye and light of step, Tabitha came down the slope at the side of the house. She had just been having a quarrel with her neighbour Bundle. Not a serious quarrel but the sort of quarrel which both sides enjoy. Bundle had hissed at her and she had hissed at Bundle and then she had trotted off home, feeling pleased with herself. She was a mackerel-grey tabby cat with alert green eyes and a chin and chest of purest white. And Tabitha was Pufftail's daughter.

Although she was only a year old, Tabitha had already given birth: to a litter of four kittens, in the previous autumn. Three of her kittens had gone to what the people who looked after her described as "good homes". And one had been retained. The people called him Kitchener because he spent so much of his time in the kitchen. He had a pink nose and bright green inquisitive eyes, a little like his mother Tabby's own. And he was a black and white cat, though largely black.

Old Father Pufftail lived in the street, but he was not a member of any human household. When it was very cold he crept through the cat-door at Number Twelve and slept in the kitchen there. Sometimes he lodged in a garden shed or a garage. But Old Father Pufftail was a proud and independent cat who called no man or woman or child his owner. He even resented being called by a name, though everyone in the street called him Pufftail; and he was, in fact, a much-loved local "character". Tabitha loved her father. She took him for granted. She did not realize how unusual it is for a cat to know their father. Kitchener's dad had visited Tabitha the previous summer from far away; and she still cherished the memory of him — a plump black tom with mysterious eyes. The evenings he had stood howling for her on the shed roof were very dear in her memory; and the warm, moonlit nights which had followed. But he was only a figure in her memory and she did not expect to see him again. Whereas Pufftail, who made such a thing of being wild, and a stray and independent, always hovered about.

Though he lived among dustbins and potting-sheds, though all his food was begged or stolen, Pufftail was every inch a gentleman – a gentleman of the road perhaps. Tabitha did not quite know the half of her father's life. She knew that people had been unkind to him and she knew that he had endured great adventures before he met Tabitha's mother. But of the details her father had told her little.

And there he sat, in the afternoon sunshine, on top of the garden wall with his grandson Kitchener, looking as sober and domestic as a neutered pedigree in a vicarage.

"Grandfather is telling me about the good old days," said Kitchener as they saw his mother approach.

"Your ears are dirty," said Tabitha, instinctively licking her son. "You'll end up looking like your grandfather if you don't wash."

"Oh, charming," said Pufftail. "You see what it is to have a loving daughter? You see why I hover about your house, with such irresistible compliments as this falling from your mother's lips?"

"What's a comp thingamy?" asked Kitchener with a look of innocence.

"It is a nice thing you say about someone," said Tabitha. "And Grandfather was making a joke. He thinks I was being rude about him."

"And were you?"

"A little," said Tabitha with a smile. "Now, Father, would you like me to go into the kitchen and see what I can see?"

"Dear girl, you are kindness itself!"

Tabitha remembered that the people who shared her house had the extravagant habit of eating only the meat on

10

lamb chops. There had been lamb chops for lunch and lots of nice fat left on the bones at the side of the people's plates. She trotted indoors to get a couple of chops for her father's supper, leaving Pufftail talking to little Kitchener. And all summer long that conversation went on. While Tabitha went about her useful tasks of making things neat, of snoozing, of bringing out food or chasing birds, or quarrelling with the neighbours, Pufftail sat at the dustbin end of the garden and told little Kitchener all about the old days. This is the story as he told it to him.

CHAPTER TWO

When you have lived as many long years in the world as I have, you too will be full of memories which you want to share; and I hope that you have a grandkitten, as I do now, who will sit patiently and listen to you! With the onset of my old age I talk too much. I know that. One of the reasons I want to tell you the story of my life, however, is to try to teach you to be brave and free and independent, for you are a cat and not a slave to any other creature in the universe. But before I begin I have to admit that there is hardly a cat to be met with in our part of the world who is not patheti-cally dependent when young upon the human race. I do hear tell that in other worlds there are wild cats who live far from the habitations of men and who lead the free and wild and unfettered life which all cats are meant to lead. But it is not like that in our world, the world of streets and houses and dustbins. Nearly all the cats who are born in that world owe their survival to the human race. Coarse, smelly, ugly creatures, they may be. But it was two-footers who had it in their power, at my birth, to drown me or to save my life; it was two-footers who brought me food and who gave my mother warmth and, although it sticks in my throat to say so, it was two-footers who decided my fate.

I do not know how long it took before we were all weaned and independent of our mother. But I think that I was about eight weeks old when the happy security of my world was for ever broken. There were to be no more long hours snuggled with some old clothes in the drawer at the bottom of the wardrobe, clinging for comfort to that most wonderful of all mothers; no more innocent little journeys downstairs in a basket, no more happy gambols in front of a burning log fire, as the kind but foolish people played with us.

It is my belief that these people were trying to find us what human beings call "good homes", for a number of two-footers came galumphing into that sitting-room to gawp at us as we played with balls of wool by the fire. I can remember with a very distinct horror the first time one of them picked me up. It was a powdery woman in spectacles with a very long nose.

"Hello, darling!" she said, holding me within an inch of her benign face. "Aren't they sweet — but no, I think my heart has really gone out to the black and white one."

So she took my sister instead. I have amused myself, many a time, by wondering what sort of a life my sister had with this kind spinster lady with the spectacles and the powdery nose. I should think that by now my sister is very comfortable and very genteel. Probably if she met me she would turn up her nose with the utmost disdain and rush indoors to her spinster-mistress with squeaks of indignation. "Squeak-squeak," she might say. "I very *nearly* came face to face with an alley-cat." So you did, my darling, so you did. For an "alley-cat" is what I am and proud of it — as you shall hear. Not for me the comfortable parlour where my sister probably, at this very moment, snoozes while her mistress watches a boring programme on the electrical picture box. Not for me the "Naughty! Mind the potted plants", whenever you feel like jumping on their ridiculous furniture. Not for me the whole horrible business of "Have you put the cat out, dear?" And then the servile little trot to the back door, the saucer of milk, before being shut up for hours in the kitchen with a litter tray. If this is civilization, you can have it. Why your mother submits to it I do not know.

One of my brothers also went to a "good home". We hardly noticed he was gone. Some children came round to have tea with the family where we lodged and at the end of the meal, after a session of quite gratifying cat worship, they walked out with a basket.

"I think they will look after him," one of the human beings said when the children were gone.

"Oh, I'm sure they will. And didn't you see the look of excitement on Giles's face?"

No, I had not seen it. But I saw the look of sadness on my mother's face late that afternoon as she paced about the sitting-room looking for my brother and my sister. After a while she gave up the search. Being a cat – as you will soon discover if you do not know it already – is a story of unending and unexplained loss. We seldom know where our lost ones are and whether they have died, or been taken, or just moved on. This was my first glimpse of the fact; the sight of my poor mother, her tail swishing (yes, I can remember the swishing of that tail, even though all her other features – her face, and her colouring – elude my memory), hunting for her children and refusing to be comforted because they were not there.

The people in whose house I was born were a man and a woman and some children. In the few days after my brother was taken away there were endless conversations about what would become of the "other two" – that is of me and my remaining brother. I really believe that they were on the verge of keeping us but the father of the household opposed the plan. It appeared that they were about to go on holiday and their house was to be occupied by some friends of theirs.

"We can't expect the Robinsons to look after *three* cats for a fortnight," he said one evening when my brother and I were sitting with our mother by the fire.

"But," said a child, "they are such dear little kittens. Please, Daddy, please let us keep them."

"That was never the idea," said the man.

"They're very sweet now," said his wife, "but think what a handful they will be when they grow into tom cats."

14

"I'd help feed them," said another child.

"It's such a pity that the Harts let us down," said the woman. "Very unreliable, the Harts. They seemed so interested in the idea when we told them Georgina was expecting."

"They decided in the end on Siamese," said the man from behind his newspaper.

I never know why human beings have this habit of holding newspapers in front of their faces but presumably it is because even human beings find each other as ugly as we find them and they wish to hide themselves.

"I think the obvious answer is to give them to a pet shop," he said from behind his newspaper-hide.

"Oh, no!" said one child.

And another said, "But Daddy."

But Daddy said, "No buts." And then he put one of those small paper chimneys between his lips and lit it and began to fill the room with an unpleasant smoky smell.

So, that evening, my brother's fate and mine was decided. We were both so young that we did not understand what the human beings were talking about. And I think our poor mother cannot have had the heart to explain to us what the discussion had meant. Recalling it now, that last night with my mother, it seems that she snuggled against us and licked us with particular tenderness. She cried a lot next morning when we were put into a basket. Till the day I die I will remember the sweet noise of my mother crying. At first my brother and I thought that we were merely being put into a basket in order to be taken downstairs to play. But this was a different kind of basket, with a sort of cage at the front. And I remember peering through the grille of that cage and looking for my mother and being unable to see her. I could only hear her plaintive voice calling to us her last sad goodbye. We never saw her again.

CHAPTER THREE

We were taken to the pet shop by the woman of the house. Evidently, she had made some previous arrangement with the pet shop man because he expressed no surprise when she entered his shop and placed the basket, with us inside, on the counter.

"Good morning, Mrs Wentworth. These are the little fellows, are they?"

"It's very sad to part with them," said Mrs Wentworth, "but I'm sure they will go to good homes."

"Oh, deary me, yes," said the pet shop man. "I never sell to anyone unless I'm quite sure they will be responsible owners. Now we have all the details, don't we? You have had them injected?"

Apparently all these so-called necessities had been gone through and we had been taken to a vet and injected against all the various diseases which human beings fear we would catch. Funnily enough, I remember nothing about it. Presumably it was in that very basket where we now sat in the pet shop. All the other memories of what has happened to me since have overlaid the trivial one of visiting a vet.

The pet shop man had a very red shiny face and in him the human smell was even stronger than in the Wentworths. It was unpleasant when he pressed this shiny red face against the bars of the basket and said, "Oh yes, they look very nice young chaps. I shall have no difficulty in selling those. And the money we agreed was satisfactory?"

Mrs Wentworth was evidently happy with the financial arrangements.

"It really will be hard to say goodbye," she said.

"You needn't worry, Madam. They will be quite safe and happy."

What foolish and untrue words these were!

With his rather lumpy fingers the pet shop man picked us out of the basket one by one by the scruff of the neck.

"This is the kindest way of handling a young cat," he said, doubtless in response to a pained expression on Mrs Wentworth's face. "I'll put them in the window, and, believe me, Madam, they'll be sold in no time."

After these words had been spoken I suppose that Mrs Wentworth slipped away taking that basket-cage with her. And at eight or nine weeks old my new life had begun.

I am a wary and suspicious character now but it was not so then. I was young and innocent. I looked at the world with large innocent green eyes and expected it all to be as comfortable and as kind as the household of the Wentworths. At first, the experience of being in the pet shop was so new and interesting that I quite forgot to be sad. The window in which my brother and I had been placed was like a sort of cage. Through the glass at one end of it we could look out at the street, and through the cage at the other we could look back into the shop. The shop smelt of seeds and hay but blending with this there was a delicious and appetizing aroma which my brother and I soon learnt to identify as mice. The mice were in a different window, at right angles to our own, but by looking across the shop we could see them. There were about ten of them being fattened up in a cage with little bowls of dried food. They were white mice with red eyes. I now consider white mice to taste insipid and much prefer the flavour of a house mouse. (Though, for true flavour, you cannot beat a brown field mouse, eaten very rapidly, soon after it has been killed.) At that stage neither my brother nor I had even thought of eating a mouse. We merely luxuriated in the smell and felt our mouths watering, as we watched the foolish little creatures in their cage scuttling about on a treadmill. There were also some gerbils and some hamsters which in my opinion are hardly worth the bother of catching. The proportion of fur to meat is decidedly unappetizing and you have to choose between taking ridiculously dainty mouthfuls and spitting out the fur in between or gulping them whole and then vomiting up the fur.

In a tank near the mouse cage there were some coloured fish, scudding about among the rocks and artificial plants with which these over-estimated delicacies are usually served in a human household. (Again, for taste, give me the great outdoors. The nicest fish I have ever eaten have been goldfish the size of kittens, scooped out of an ornamental pond in a garden.)

In spite of this range of tasty delicacies within our view, my brother and I were merely given some rather nasty little biscuits by the shop man. Once Mrs Wentworth had gone his tone became distinctly more surly.

"You take your eyes off my fish or I'll skin yer," he said to us rudely.

"Skin you!" echoed a loud screeching voice. "Skin you." It was a green parrot, which was kept in a cage, unhygienically near the bins of bran and rabbit food.

"Shut your face," said the man. "The same goes for you."

"Skin you," shouted back the intrepid parrot.

"Hello, sonny," said the shop man in quite a different voice, an oily ingratiating voice. "What can I do for you?"

A boy had come into the shop.

"Got any lizards?" he asked.

"No," said the man. "We're right out of lizards at the moment. Hoping to get some more in next week, but just at the moment there's a shortage."

"Only, I wanted a green one," said the boy.

"Like I say," said the man, "we're hoping to get some in next week. Now, mice. We've got some lovely mice."

"I don't want a mouse," said the boy. "I want a green lizard."

"Ever had a lizard before, have you?" asked the man.

"Not exactly," said the boy cautiously.

"Only they're not that easy to handle," said the man. "A lizard's not like a mouse. Easy, mice is. And friendly. You wouldn't call a lizard friendly."

"Can I look at the mice?" asked the boy.

"You go ahead, sonny, and look at the mice."

The boy went and stared at the cage where the mice, so tantalizingly, were scampering about, and running around in their treadmill.

"My sister's scared of mice," he said contemptuously.

"Is she now?"

"I think it's silly to be scared of mice."

"Very silly," said the man. "They make ever such friendly little pets, and looking after them's no trouble. The cages are cheap too. Got a lot of new cages in, as a matter of fact."

"Do you really think it would be easy to look after a mouse?"

"Cinch," said the man. "Easy as pie, mice is. Not like lizards, which are really more of a handful than you'd think. They gets diseases, and that."

"Don't mice get diseases?"

"Mice? Nar! Still, if you want an expensive, difficult lizard, rather than a nice, cheap, easy little mouse, I wouldn't stand in your way. But, you know what I'd do?"

"Skin you!" shouted the parrot.

"No," said the boy. "What would you do?"

"I'd buy a mouse," said the man.

"She really squeals at the mention of mice," said the boy excitedly, reverting to his sister. "How much are they?"

"Normally they're a pound," said the man, "but for a first time buyer like yourself, I'd go down to fifty pence."

"I've saved up ten pounds," said the boy. "I thought I'd buy a lizard and a tank and rocks and everything."

"Well, I'm glad you mentioned the money, in that case," said the man. "'Cause a lizard tank and all the equipment would set you back a tenner for a start, before you even bought yer lizard. Whereas, I can let you have this nice little cage here for a fiver."

"Could you really?" said the boy.

"Five pounds for a nice cage," said the man.

"Then I'd have five pounds left," said the boy. "I've been saving up for a year. I'd saved seven pounds, and then my granny gave me three pounds for my birthday. We thought lizards were cheaper than that."

"Not with the equipment," said the man.

"I think I'd better buy a mouse cage," said the boy, who was staring at the white mice in fascination.

"I think you're very wise," said the man. "You just wait a minute and I'll —"

"Skin you!" said the parrot again.

— "get one down from the shelf."

In the end he sold the boy the cage, two mice ("They'll get edgy on their own."), a treadmill, a little mirror, a feeding bowl and a bag of food. He gave the boy one pound change out of his ten pounds.

"There we are, Polly," laughed the man when the boy had left the shop. "Another satisfied customer. I've had those mice on my hands for months. They've been looking peaky. Wouldn't be surprised if they didn't pop off in a month or two."

My brother and I sat in the window all morning looking sometimes out at the street and sometimes back into the shop. Customers came in and out. On the whole they were less gullible than the little boy and came in to buy specific objects: five pound bags of rabbit food, dog leashes, worming powder, flea collars, bird seed or fish food.

Passers-by on the pavement outside the shop peered in at us. If we jumped up and pressed our paws against the glass, begging them not to stare, they stared at us all the more. Our presence there constituted quite a little side-show. In the afternoon some children came in and asked how much we were. The shop man said we were five pounds each. They asked if they could stroke us and were told only if they were serious. Evidently they weren't serious at all for they soon let us be.

By evening we were both feeling rather hungry. We had been spoilt, I suppose, by the Wentworths. I had grown used to thinking that minced liver and scrambled egg and fresh milk were foods to be expected automatically. But all we had that day was a bowl of biscuits and a dish of water. When darkness had fallen the man told the parrot that he was going to lock up the shop and we, with the other animals, were left alone in our prison.

"We've been in here long enough," said my brother. "I wonder where mother is. When do you think they will be taking us back to mother?"

"I don't know," said I. "But I suspect that..."

But when I looked at my brother's questioning face, I could not voice my suspicions. He had obviously not been thinking as I had been. For him, this tedious business of being locked up in a pet shop window was just some kind of boring game. Sooner or later, we would be released and life would return to normal. We did not realize (I myself could not realize it fully) that there would never again be a "normal" to which life might return; and that for ever afterwards we would be pressing on, with the world our enemy, into new and strange adventures.

Let me describe my brother to you. When I look at you, little black-and-white Grandkitten, I am quite reminded of him. From the beginning he was a handsome cat with a good thick coat of black fur. His face and chest, however, were white and so were his paws, white about half-way up the legs, as though he were wearing boots of human kind. Hence the "name" which they ignominiously imposed upon him. You call me simply by the name of grandfather but you know as well as any cat that we do not have names, any more than the Gods themselves have names. The habit of naming is a human one. Men think that when they have named something, they have subdued it. Even our great Mother-of-Night and all her handmaidens and concubines

21

and sisters, whom we know as nameless guardians and friends as we pace the roof-tops by night, these divinities the human race call stars. But with us it is not so. We do not, as they do, wish to possess all that we conquer, nor to subdue all that we admire. We are content to allow things to be themselves, from the highest Gods to the smallest mice, and without imposing upon them our own naming. That is why we are without names. My brother will always be my brother but for me he is the brother without name and until the point in the story where it seems right to use the foolish name which human beings bestowed upon him, I will not sully my lips by using it.

But, as I began, let me finish and let me describe my brother. He was black and white. His markings were as I described and his eyes were of the very brightest green. We were both large kittens for our age; but I think that my brother was even larger than I. We did not much resemble each other. My face, gazing back at me from mirrors and windows and puddles of water and ponds, has always worn a scowl. His face was peaceful and innocent. My tail has always been a thick matted affair – hence the "name" by which "they" call me now. But his tail was straight and sleek and purely black, only curling when he moved or felt excitement or fear.

From now on, after we had left my mother's care, my brother and I were not just brothers. We were friends. Neither of us knew what the future held and neither of us, quite, understood what a shop was. I know that it had not occurred to us that we might be separated. I merely feared that we had been brought here for some incomprehensible human purpose and that we would never return home. That was why, when he asked me if we would soon be returning to our mother, I did not have the heart to tell him my fears.

"The food here's pretty boring," said my brother. "The bloke forgot to bring our meat."

"Do you really think he forgot?"

"Surely, brother. Did you not hear him promise Mrs

Wentworth that he would look after us, and that we would be safe and happy?"

"Oh yes," I said with a sad heart. "I had forgotten that. Silly of me."

"This cage is small, isn't it?"

"Yes."

"I could do with a nice run about."

"So could I."

"Do you think we could get through that clear stuff if we pushed hard enough with our paws?"

"The clear stuff which we both see and don't see and which divides us from outside?" I asked. "No, you can't get through that. We tried this afternoon. Don't you remember?"

"I'm going to have one more try," said my brother. And he went to the window and jumped against it with his paws. The action attracted the attention of some people passing by on the pavement outside. A young human male with its mate stood there gawping at us. They had both covered their skin with that tight rough blue cloth which they name denim and the poor scraps of fur which they have at the top of their heads had, in the male's case, been cut short. In the female's it had been allowed to grow over her shoulders. I noticed that the female claws in a human being can be much longer and redder than the male's. She was reaching into their portable food-trough which is made of the same newspaper-substance which they use during the day for hiding their faces and bringing out strips of potato dripping with fat.

"Inny sweet?" she said, nuzzling against the male's shoulder.

"Norruz sweetuz yew," he said.

"I say, I say!" called my dear innocent brother. "You couldn't possibly... I mean, if there *is* a way out? We're new here, you see."

"Evsa toiny inny?" said the female.

"That's just it," said the male, with a portion of potato

23

still in his mouth. "Tiny now, but what's he going to grow into – see what I mean?"

"Is he mewing? I think he's mewing."

"No."

"Please, please," said my brother. "If you do happen to know the way out..."

"It's no use," I said, "they can't understand you."

"You know granny's looking for a cat," said the female. "Ever since Sammy died she's been, you know, thinking about it."

"What? Your nana is it?"

"Yes."

"Don't need to buy her a cat from a shop, do you? You can get a cat free. Put up a card in your local post offiice."

"He's evsa sweet, though, inny?" said the female.

And then we saw the back part of the female pressed against the glass while he kissed her. I suppose the mating habits of other species are always hard to understand; none more so than that of the human beings. After a bit of wiggling about they climbed into one of those mobile red things – bus is the word – and disappeared into the night. Soon after that, I suppose, I fell asleep. When I woke a few hours later all that had happened in the previous day had been obliterated by sleep. I thought I was home again, in the bottom drawer of a wardrobe with my mother. I reached out for her and clutched for her, with my eyes still shut, quite certain that I would soon feel her paw around me and that I would be gathered to her breast. But as I reached out I felt only an emptiness in the darkness; and then the small, sleepy figure of my brother. "Mummy!" I called. And then the smell of the pet shop reminded me where I was.

"Silly boy," shouted the parrot.

"What was that?" said my brother.

In their cage the mice were twittering, doubtless complaining about the way the parrot woke them up all night.

"I'm lonely," I said.

My brother tried to comfort me by licking his paw and

wiping my face with it, the way that mother used to do. But it was no substitute. The gesture, which both reminded me of mother and brought home to me the hopelessness of our situation, was merely a source of pain.

"Gosh, I miss her," he said, clutching me tightly.

"So do I," said I. And there we lay, on the hard floor of the shop window, until morning light began to appear.

CHAPTER FOUR

The futile routine of the pet shop resumed when we had been awake for some hours. The man, who had sleeked the fur on top of his head with even more grease than the previous day's supply, arrived just at the moment when I thought I might actually be dying of starvation. It was agony to watch him waddling round the shop, first checking that all his merchandise were alive; then cleaning the cages, with many an oath and curse – as though, for his convenience, the animal kingdom might learn to digest its food without any waste product coming out at the other end.

"Look at all this you done," he said crossly to the mice. "Who'da thought it?" Subserviently, the eight remaining mice squeaked their apologies. The smell of them, droppings and all, wafted across to our cage; and to my hungry nostrils it was very beautiful. I could have eaten all eight for my breakfast that morning. I could have eaten the parrot too, and it would have done my heart good before eating it to sink my teeth into its squeaking throat and stop its silly clamour, "Silly boy, silly boy."

"You watch who you're talking to," said the pet shop man.

When he came over to our cage he said, "Bloomin' 'ek. You're nearly as bad. I hate the smell of cat. Sooner I'm rid of you two the better. It were a mistake buying you. A pound I paid for you two – fifty pence each! You'll have eaten fifty pence worth o' biscuits if you stay here much longer." And he gave us another saucerful of unappetizing biscuits and a little tin saucer of water.

As it happened several people came into the shop asking

about us but he either tried to be too greedy (at that stage we cost five pounds each) or his manner put them off. A couple more of the mice got sold and a plastic bag of water containing two of the most doleful goldfish I ever saw in my life. But we weren't sold. When he gave us our afternoon biscuits the man said, "I don't know. If it goes on like this I shall have to drown you, I will really." Neither my brother nor I knew whether he was joking.

When I look back on our time in the shop window, I admire the confident way in which my brother and I assumed that we would always be together. In the previous week our litter of four had been broken up and we had been separated from our mother. But I never really imagined that this final, cruel separation could have taken place. It was he who first thought of it, after we had finished our lunch.

"If you're taken first, I hope you get fixed up with a decent place," he said.

"Eh?"

"You know. If someone comes in and takes you before I'm taken," he said.

"Do you think that's likely to happen?" I asked.

"They could take either of us first," he said.

"No, I mean that they will separate us?"

"Oh, brother," he said sadly, "hadn't you realized?"

I have often thought of those words and I have thought of the way in which he then said, so sadly, and, for one so young, so wisely, "Do you remember what mother used to say? 'A cat is always alone, especially when he is in company.'"

These thoughts made me very sad indeed. In fact they turned me into a complete cry-baby and I nuzzled against my brother for comfort. I was still in this unhappy posture when he nudged me and said, "Listen. I think this is it!"

How my stomach turned at the thought that my solitary life was about to begin. I was not ready for it! I was too young! And in spite of what our dear mother used to say, a cat is *not* always alone. We are, in fact, sociable beasts, and to live in total solitude with only human companionship is a recipe for feline unhappiness.

"They're lovely, and no mistake," said a kindly old female voice. "Wasn't it lucky my granddaughter saw them? She was passing by your window last night with Bob – he's her young man. They're courting, you know. This morning she come to me and said, 'Granny, you know how we's always telling you how you ought to have a cat? Well, there's two ever such nice ones down the pet shop.' 'Not all the way down the High Street,' I said. 'However d' you expect me to get all the way down there with my ankles and getting on and off a bus at my age...'"

I expect that, though so young, you have already noticed that some human beings make noises with their mouths almost all the time. When they sleep their mouths and noses make an ugly grunting noise. And when they are awake they jabber. Granny Harris jabbered but she did so quite pleasantly. The pet shop man found it hard to get a word in between her flow of talk.

"Well, he's working, Bob is, that's Tracy's intended, I say intended, they aren't exactly engaged, well people aren't so much nowadays are they, it's all different, but you know, regular work, so if they got the money why not enjoy themselves, so they come out and saw a film, and came home afterwards. That's when they saw the kittens."

Granny Harris turned and peered at us through the bars.

"Aren't you lovely?" she said.

She had a round, jolly face and very bright blue eyes, white hair tied back in a bun, on top of which a hat was perched, fixed by a hat-pin. She looked a very old-fashioned lady indeed.

"The black and white one's gorgeous," she said.

My poor brother gave me a "look".

"But then so's the tabby. You know I can't decide."

"Difficult, innit? They're both such *darlings*," said the pet shop man, leering at us. Could he tell, from the looks of absolute disdain with which we answered him, how much we loathed and already despised him?

"Perhaps I shouldn't really get either," Granny Harris suddenly said. "It's a bit of an extravagance buying a cat, isn't it? And who knows? People are always trying to find homes for kittens aren't they, and an awful lot just get given away. Mind you, it isn't right the way some people treat cats, it's terrible really the things you read nowadays, what with cruelty to animals, and laboratories, and hunting otters."

"I so agree with you, Madam," said the shop man in his smarmiest voice. "You know, that's why I think it's a good thing to charge a small sum of money for a pet. Left to me, I'd give 'em away free – all these lovely animals: the mice over there, the parrot, the fish. But if I give 'em away, am I sure the person really wants the pet, really wants to care for it? Know what I mean?"

"I think you may be right," said Granny Harris.

"I mean it's criminal, the way some people treats their pets. And I couldn't agree with you more. But if they'd had to pay just a little bit for their pet in the first place, they'd think twice about whether they really wanted it."

"I never thought of that," said Granny Harris.

"I mean, take yourself, Madam. You're a very responsible person, a very thoughtful, caring person."

"Am I really?" smiled Granny Harris.

"You haven't just picked up the first cat that came along. You've thought it through, you've talked it over with your family – with whom you obviously enjoy a very good relationship..."

None of this was exactly true. Tracy had promised that she would do some shopping for her grandmother, and that she would deliver it that morning. Instead she had rung Granny Harris to say that she wouldn't be doing it after all, why didn't the old woman go into town herself? The exercise would do her good and while she did her shopping, she could look in the pet shop window and see those sweet little kittens.

But as the pet man spoke it seemed to Granny Harris as if everything he said was true and she wanted it to be true. And her purely impulsive decision to have a look at the kittens truly felt as if it had come about as a result of hard thinking and a warm, friendly discussion with all her family.

"A cat's company," she said. "That's what I think. Aren't you beautiful?" she said to me.

"Oh, there's no question about it," said the pet man. "Left to myself, I'd keep these little chaps myself. I would really."

I prayed to all the Gods that he was lying.

"It would be quite safe to have a cat with a budgie, would you say?" asked Granny Harris.

"A budgie?"

"Yes. It's a green budgie," she said, as though the colour could affect the issue one way or another.

"Funnily enough," said the man, "I've known a lot of customers who've had a budgie and a cat or the other way around and they've often been very good friends. You get cat owners coming back for new budgies – oh, very frequently."

"*New* budgies?" she asked suspiciously.

"Well, any age you like," he said. "What I mean is, there won't be any trouble. None whatsoever. In fact, it'll enhance your budgie's life. Blue was it?"

"Green. He can't speak, but he can chirrup. He got out of his cage once and flew right up onto the telegraph wires. Mind you," she said, staring at us intently, "it's difficult to know which one..."

"It all depends really," said the pet man, "on how much you were thinking of spending."

"I'm only on the pension," said Granny shrewdly.

"Well, the cat's the cheapest thing you could buy – for the

money," emphasized the shop man, as though some people perhaps bought things with some other convertible commodity – teeth, beads, potatoes. "I mean it's an investment."

For you and me, Grandkitten, who have never had money and who have always taken what we needed but never more than we needed, the human attitude to possessions and riches will always be mysterious. If you go up into the middle of the town you will find whole houses devoted to nothing but money – saving it, borrowing it, hoarding it up and taking it out in little bits, lending it. They queue up in these houses – which they call banks and building societies – day after day. They go in and mutter about money to the priests of the cult and pay their dues so that they can borrow or lend more of it. On either side of the banks and building societies are the shops and everything that you can see in their windows – all the clothes and the tinned food and the journeys to places in the sun, all the carpets and sofas and fur trimmings and miniature paper chimneys – are paid for with the borrowed money which the priests have given to the people from the Bank-Temples. And that is why the shop man was offering us for sale, like slaves. The highest praise which he could heap upon us was to say that we were an "investment", which is what they call the offerings they make to the bank-priests from their own hoards.

"Dear me," said Granny Harris, "I *have* only got a pension."

"Now these cats here might look to you like any ordinary moggy," he said, staring at me contemptuously, "and any ordinary black and white. But in point of fact, they is pedigree. Rare breeds, these. They cost me all of a fiver each and by the time I reckon how much it's cost me to feed them, keep them – they've been fed on nothing but the best meat, dear —"

"Well, I just wanted an ordinary cat," said Granny, "nothing expensive, nothing pedigree."

"That's just what I was going to say," said the shop man.

"Though they are in fact highly pedigree, the nice thing about these two is that they aren't in the least difficult. If you bought one of these you'd in fact be buying a pedigree, but getting what is a very nice, reassuring pedigree cat."

"How much? I couldn't pay five pounds," she said.

"There's others would," said the man.

"Is there? You can get cats free. I could put up a card, like I said, and get a kitten free. I could go down the Animal Sanctuary and get one. Just that you're nearer, and you've got the cats. Shame, though," she said, making a pleasant face. "I've quite taken a fancy to him." And she made a cooing gesture towards my brother and, gathering herself together, she waddled out of the shop, dragging along her basket on wheels behind her.

"Wait!" said the pet shop man. "Please wait, Madam."

"Good day to you, Sir," said Granny, purposefully, and made her way off down the High Street.

"Pedigree!" yelled the parrot.

"Yeah," said the man, "well how was I to know. I thought she'd be a sucker."

"I think she was going to take me on my own," said my brother. "It was a lucky escape."

There were several enquiries after us in the course of the morning but each customer shook his or her head when they heard that we cost five pounds each. All made the same response. You could pick up an ordinary moggy (that was me!) for nothing, so why waste a fiver on "it"?

At dinner time, the pet shop man locked his shop, and returned, an hour later, smelling strongly of a mixture of beer, whisky, cheese and pickles.

"At this rate, I'm going to have you on my hands for ever," he said crossly. "And I tell you straight my friends," – at this he brought his shiny, malodorous face close to the bars – "if you haven't been sold by tomorrow, I'm going to drown you!"

This did not do much for the spirits of either my brother

32

or myself, as we got through another twelve hours in the window. We ate a few more platefuls of biscuits. We watched a few more silly children buy a few more mice. We watched as more people stared at us through the glass of the window. And once more, when he had locked up the shop and departed for home, with the maledictions of the parrot echoing behind him, we spent our lonely night in confinement.

You are a young cat and you have never been locked up. You probably can't imagine what it is like to be locked up for hours and hours. I notice how frisky you get when your people have shut you in the kitchen for the night. But that is a large room with curtains to swing from, butter to lick and china on the dresser to wobble and play with. Above all, you have space to run about. But it was not so with us. We were two young kittens with all the friskiness and energy which you have now. And for two whole days we had been shut up in a space about the size of the top of your kitchen table. It increased our dejection.

Moreover, we were both very young and we believed everything which was said to us. The threat that, if we were not sold soon, we would be drowned, was very real to us. We were too tired and too sad and too young to know what we would be missing if indeed we were killed tomorrow. So far, life had been at first intensely delightful and then almost as acutely miserable. Memories of the delights were fading; it would have been good to bring the misery to an end. And yet there was something within me which resisted the idea of death and I knew that if that man tried to lay his filthy hands on me and kill me, I would not go to my death unresisting. Lying there, with my head on my brother's shoulder, I plotted how I would sink my teeth into the man's hand, or scratch his face. Vain ambitions! He could have wrung my neck with the smallest twist.

It was raining the next day when we woke. I can remember the bad temper of the shop man when he arrived and fumbled with the keys. We got quite sprayed with rain-water as he shook out his mackintosh and cloth cap and cursed the English climate.

"Early closing today," he said to us unpleasantly. "And I warn you. If you haven't been sold by dinner time ..." and he made dramatic gestures by putting both his hands round his neck and pretending to strangle himself. I could tell that he was extremely discomfited to be found in the middle of this display by Granny Harris who rattled at that moment on the glass of the door with her umbrella.

"Are you open?" she said.

"Not till nine," replied the man.

"It's five to nine now, and you are there and I am here, so will you please open up this shop?" she said.

And realizing that she was a potential customer, he let her in once more.

"I went home and didn't sleep a wink all night just for thinking about him," she said.

"The moggy?"

"The black and white!" she said. "I've been worried, in spite of all you said yourself, about having a cat with a budgie. I asked my neighbour if she'd ever heard that a cat gets on well with a budgie and she said she'd never heard such *sales* talk. Ask him, she says, how a budgie gets on with a cat!"

"Well then," said the man, "I don't know your neighbour but I do think I can speak with the voice of experience and, if I may say so, authority..."

"But I stayed awake all night thinking of his sad face."

"The budgie's?"

"No, no, that beautiful black and white creature in the window, with his big white boots and I thought to myself, he'll see me out and he'll be a good companion to me in my old age and if I can't keep a budgie's cage locked against Bootsie, I don't deserve a cat or budgie."

"Bootsie, you call him?"

"That's what he's called," said Granny, staring senti-mentally at my brother.

My brother and I exchanged glances of consternation. It had never occurred to either of us that a human being could have the arrogance to call us by a name – still less such a silly name as Bootsie. But in this claim on my brother, we realized a much worse thing. She really was going to buy him and we were about to be parted for ever.

"Well, old boy," said my brother, "it looks as though we're going to have to say goodbye."

"She seems decent," I said, "better than..." We did not have a name for the pet shop man but my brother knew whom I meant.

"Much," he said. "I just hope you find a decent person soon. You needn't worry. He won't..."

"Kill me? What makes you so sure?"

"He'll want the money." My brother had apprehended more of human nature than I had.

"But I'm only a moggy," I said. "And they can get cats like me without paying any money. I think I'm for it."

Granny Harris was saying, "What would an old body like me be wanting with all the equipment? A cat basket? What's wrong with the basket I've got here, a basket on wheels if ever a basket was? Rubber bones is it now? And what's that? Cat chocolates!"

Evidently the man was trying to persuade her that in order to look after my brother properly, she needed to spend five or ten pounds on useless junk in his pet shop.

We had missed the earlier part of the conversation, so evidently, she had agreed to buy my brother. But then the shop man said sharply, "Please yourself. I tell you what I'm going to do, and it isn't something I'd do for everyone. For an extra couple of quid I'll throw in the moggy."

"But I don't want two cats."

"Two cats is easier than one," said the man. "They make company for themselves. It isn't kind having just the one."

"It's the black and white I want and it's the black and white I'll take," said Granny Harris, who was evidently finding the man's attempt to charm as irksome as we did.

"One pound extra," said the man. "And if you don't like him after a week, you can bring him back."

"And what makes you so interested to get rid of him, I should like to know?" said Granny. "What was all that yesterday about his being pedigree and an expensive breed? No, you keep your moggy and I'll buy my black and white."

The man opened the cage and reached into the window for my brother, who was snatched up before I had the chance to say goodbye to him. With very little ceremony, I saw him being dumped into Granny's basket. It was the sort of basket with a top which strapped down with buckles. I stood on my hind legs and called out to him.

"Goodbye! Goodbye!"

"Oh," said Granny. "Just look at that cat!"

"I'll never forget you," I called. "And who knows, we might meet again."

"Goodbye!" my brother called from the basket.

"Ah!" said Granny. "They're mewing for each other." And then she poked the shop man with the handle of her umbrella and said, "Bother you. I wouldn't be surprised if you didn't train them to do it. I'll give you a pound for the moggy."

"Done," said the man.

"I don't really want him," said Granny Harris.

But within five minutes, I was next to my brother once again, feeling his grateful heart pounding against my own, as in the darkness of Granny Harris's shopping basket, we bounced and trundled along the High Street towards the bus stop, at that moment two of the happiest cats in the world.

CHAPTER FIVE

My brother and I lived together with Mrs Harris for about two years as human beings measure the passage of our Mother-of-Night. And if you ask me how I know it is easy to tell you. When we went to live with Granny Harris there were a few daffodils sprouting in the yard by her back door. And then they faded and disappeared. And then they reappeared a year later and faded and went. It was when they reappeared a second time that our life began to change.

Those were happy years on the whole. Granny Harris lived in a small terraced house on the eastern side of the town. Downstairs there was a tiny little front room, a tiny little back room and a scullery. Upstairs, there was her bedroom, and another bedroom, always empty, a bathroom, and in the bathroom that well they sit on for getting rid of their business.

Nowadays, I feel no desire for a regular human habitation, such as you have, little kitten. I am happy enough to get my kip wherever the fancy takes me. If it is a warm day I often find myself falling asleep on your garden wall while you and your mother play on the grass down below. When it rains there are not a few garden sheds up and down the street where I can take refuge. Some cats I know sleep in garages but my heart is made sick by the sight of the engines of murder which people store there and by the smell of the liquid which they pour into them. On very cold nights, when the world becomes white and hard and our Mother-of-Night shines brightly above us, I sometimes push through the cat-door and sleep in the kitchen at Number Twelve and lie by the warm cupboard there. But night is no time to sleep. The hunting is better at night and no food tastes as good as the food you have caught yourself.

But in those far-off days we were happy enough, my brother and I, to lodge in Granny Harris's house. She had had a cat before, whom she called Sammy; and her son-in-law Jim had put a little cat-flap into her back door to enable Sammy to get in and out of the yard without disturbing her. For our first few months there she kept us locked up in the kitchen at nights. But when we were old enough she let us roam free and we began to experience the delights of the chase.

My brother was an expert hunter. I will never forget the excitement, one dawn, of catching our first thrush. We were playing in the yard, practising fisticuffs, when he suddenly froze and hissed to me between his teeth, "Look! Look, there!"

On the other side of the yard, only a few feet away from us, a plump male thrush was cracking the shell of its break-fast snail. It was a magnificent bird, with speckled plumage on its breast and nut-brown feathers on its back and tail. The task of cracking the snail was so absorbing that it did not seem to notice us staring at it. You know the excitement – your whole body tingling with the thrill of it, your fur on edge, your heartbeat quickened; though as yet, Grandson, you are too impulsive and you miss too many chances. My brother taught me the importance of absolute stillness and patience.

Hammer, hammer, hammer!

The thrush had its back to us. Neither of us said a word. We communed silently. At exactly the right moment my brother pounced, with claws out, and cuffed the bird on the side of its head. He had been so swift that it still had the snail in its beak when he knocked it off its legs. The bird began to flap and squeak but by then I had pounced on it and bitten one of its wings so that it could not fly away. Then, after the first excitement of the chase, there came the glorious surge of blood-lust. It is a wonderful feeling, isn't it, the knowledge that you have the bird completely in your power, the certainty that soon you are going to be feasting on some warm really fresh meat. At this stage, the desire to delay the moment of the actual kill is irresistible. I know that some *people*, especially children, consider this part of the sport cruel. They are fine ones to talk about cruelty! Now that I am old and know of what cruelty people are capable, I think there was something pretty innocent about the pleasure my brother and I took in tormenting that bird. It tried to fly but because I had almost torn off one wing, it couldn't, so the more it flapped, the more hopeless its situation became. Then it hopped about despondently on its curious scaly little legs until my brother cuffed it again. I was just about to plunge my teeth into its neck when my brother said "No! We can get a few more runs out of it yet." So we withdrew a few feet, giving the poor silly creature the impression that it was free – though I don't know what sort of freedom it imagined itself possessing with a broken wing and two young cats looking down on it. Then it tried hopping across the flagstones of the yard and we descended on it again, teasing it with our paws and growling and breathing on it. Then, very suddenly, we decided to end it all. When it was limp and still we began our feast.

The blood was delicious but after a few careful mouthfuls (and I couldn't help swallowing some feathers) my brother paused.

"Our First Blood," he said proudly. "Hadn't we better tell the old woman?"

"Will she be pleased?" I asked.

"Pleased? I should say! Think of how pleased she was when Jim got – what was it called? Promotion? And when Tracy got those things."

"CSEs," said I; as you will have noticed I have a curiously retentive memory for the things people say.

"Those are the things," said my brother. "Don't know what they are, do you?"

"No idea," I said.

But they are things people like getting, like money and engines of murder.

"Well," I said, "perhaps we ought to show her our thrush." I coughed a little bit, having swallowed more feathers than was good for me.

My brother took the stiff still thrush in his mouth and led the way back into the house through the cat-flap. We went into the small tiled hall and up the stairs, and stood outside Mrs Harris's door. We could hear from her room those loud noises which human beings make when they are asleep. I think they do it because for some reason they don't know how to keep their mouths shut at the same time as sleeping. Strange creatures they are!

Mrs Harris's door was ajar and I pushed it open with my nose. By now, I had become completely convinced by my brother that there could be few things which would give the old lady more pleasure than to be woken up early in the morning in order to be presented with a dead bird. So I jumped on to her bed with great confidence and began to claw the eiderdown impatiently. As soon as the snoring stopped, I put my nose against hers and said, "Wake up, Mrs Harris, ma'am, you'll never guess what we've brought you."

"Bless us, what are you miaowing about so early in the morning?" she asked. "Hungry already? Eaten all the lovely Katto-tin I put out for you last night?"

Then my brother jumped up and dropped the thrush on her sheet and we stood back proudly, awaiting her delighted congratulations. But, you see, this is where human beings are really extraordinary. Instead of being pleased, Mrs Harris let out a little squeal of horror.

"Oh, you *naughty* boys!" she said. With great indignation she elbowed herself up into a sitting position among the pillows. "That *poor* little thrush! How could you do such a cruel thing? And it's dirty, too, I shouldn't wonder, fleas and that, like *Her* Opposite always feeding the pigeons and they

40

do say she even has pigeons in the house bringing in filth and *fleas*."

"We thought you'd like it," said my brother, really very crestfallen.

"There's no good you miaowing at me, young man, I'm very cross with you. And you," she said, shaking her finger at me.

I had meant to put up an eloquent defence of my brother's action. I was going to point out to Granny Harris that First Blood was one of the proudest moments in a young cat's life. I was going to say that people ate meat and although I didn't know how they got hold of it, I shouldn't be surprised if they didn't employ cats to procure it for them. Eating meat and then complaining that hunting was cruel was pure hippo— hippo— something. I knew there was a word for making a great song and dance of condemning the very things which you like doing yourself – a word apart from *human* that is. Hippo-something. But at that stage I couldn't think of it, for the feathers which had stuck in my gullet came satisfyingly up through my throat. I leaned forward and started to choke and then – the truly delicious sensation of vomiting.

"And now you're being sick all over my bedroom floor," said Granny Harris, "like Her Opposite's lodger, so-called, who comes home swaying like a ship in a stormy sea of a Friday night. And it serves you *right*, young man."

I have never got the hang of this human idea that being sick is something bad. True, it is not so reliably enjoyable as eating, hunting or making love, but I would rank it as one of the very highest pleasures in life. But Granny Harris considered that being sick, far from being one of the incidental pleasures of my First Blood, was some sort of punishment which I had brought upon myself. She heaved herself off the bed and shooed us out of the room.

"Off, out, the pair of you," she said. And we were banished to the garden while she cleared up. At first I supposed that she merely intended to mop up my vomit (and I did very much regret having been sick on her bedroom carpet). But after a few minutes the back door opened and we saw her come out into the garden wearing a dressing-gown. She was carrying the thrush we had killed in a little dust-pan.

"Would you *believe* it," said my brother. "She's going to bury it."

"I thought the least she could do would be to eat it for breakfast," I said. "Really, they are..."

"Extraordinary."

These last four words became a sort of catch-phrase or joke between my brother and me, and whenever we caught ourselves being once more amazed by an example of human eccentricity one of us would start up, "Really!" and the other would chime in, "they are extraordinary!" And we found this hilariously amusing. When we find something sublimely funny, we shut our eyes and swish our tails and smile. We don't go in for this heaving of the shoulders and barking that the human race do when something tickles their childish humour.

CHAPTER SIX

Well, our First Blood had one good consequence anyway, and that was that Granny Harris decided to get rid of her budgie. Compared with open-faced beautiful creatures like robins or thrushes, I even then considered the budgerigar an ill-favoured specimen of bird life, with its flat face and squashed up little beak. I am fairly sure that Granny Harris had tired of this creature after she had decided that it had nothing to say for itself.

People, you will discover, consider themselves the only creatures in the universe capable of communication, and unless you ape their particular set of noises they think you can't "talk", as they call it. An idiot parrot who can be taught to screech "skin you!" is thought to be very clever. Two house-martins calling to each other the exact directions of how to get from London to East Africa are dismissed as "dumb creatures" who are "only twittering". Well, the budgerigar could "only go tweet tweet" as far as Granny Harris was concerned. And she announced that she did not want any "trouble" for it from us. So it was decided that her daughter June should have it instead, and one day June and her husband Jim came to collect it.

My brother took an instant dislike to June and Jim, and so did I. I do not need to explain to you that there *are* some people that one knows to avoid. Jim and June were perfectly harmless. They were never going to torture us or knowingly make life a misery. But they were aliens, whom we shunned. Whenever they made one of their rare visits to the house, my brother and I always conveniently vanished.

On this occasion, June picked me up and held me in the air.

"You wouldn't eat a budgie, Fluffie, would you?" she said.

Being waved in the air makes me sick, even without looking into June's face. It is a very moist face – or it was. Whether she is still alive, I neither know nor care. It is a sort of pinky brown, and she has put paint around her eyes and her lips. How she can stand the agony of it I do not understand.

"Oh, Fluffie, Fluffie, Fluffie!" she exclaimed. "You wouldn't hurt a budgie, would you? Not my mum's budgie?"

Well yes, I have to admit that they called me Fluffie. I have concealed it from you until now. My brother was Bootsie, because he had a black body and white legs. And I was Fluffie! Just think of it. Your own grandfather, Fluffie. This Pufftail nickname they all call me by in the street is bad enough. I will not answer to it or acknowledge it. But at least it *is* only a nickname, used by people who know no better – what's that? Yes, yes, and by some cats too – because they do not know my name, and they do not realize that I, like all cats, am a creature of no name. But, Fluffie! While June was waving me in the air and saying that if I would eat the budgie I would be a naughty-wauty little diddums (that silly way they talk to animals and children, some people), Jim was telling her not to be so daft. And then she asked him whether he wanted to see mum's budgie killed by a couple of cats, and he had said that it was his idea, not hers, that they should take the budgie. And she had disputed this, and soon they were having one of their regular set-tos. That was my real reason for disliking Jim and June; the endless arguing about *everything*. It made their company pretty tedious.

I haven't really described June to you apart from that moist, painted face. She had blue fur on top of her head, hardened into a sort of helmet shape. Jim had almost no fur at all. His fur-style reminded me of the pet shop man, where we suffered our first imprisonment. What little fur he had

44

was swept back and oiled. Jim and June both smoked the paper chimneys quite a lot, too.

"Left to me, I'd drown the whole blooming lot of them," said Jim, "I mean – animals! Is it worth all the fuss?"

"You're the one making a fuss, not me."

"I like that."

During these ding-dongs, June's mother, Granny Harris, kept absolutely quiet, and said nothing. But she did eventually ask, "Well – are you taking the budgie or aren't you?" And Jim and June took it.

They did not call again on Granny Harris for weeks – months perhaps. They rarely did. When she had a few words with the milkman, or with the lady next door with the horrible children, or even, on days when she was desperately lonely, with Her Opposite, Mrs Harris would imply to them that she saw her family all the time. While we frolicked on the pavement outside her house, or in the backyard, we would hear her giving long descriptions of what Jim and June were up to: how Jim was now the manager of whatever it was he worked for, and how their child was shaping up. I am sure that my mother, if she is still alive, is not telling her neighbours all about me. It is not natural for parents to take an interest in their children, and I do not believe that Granny Harris really took any interest in June and Jim. She always seemed quite glad when they had gone. But she had to behave as if her life revolved around them. It is so silly.

What's that? Why, if I think like that, do I take so much interest in Tabitha? Your mother is a very remarkable cat, that is why. There are other reasons, which perhaps, if I ever finish telling you the story of my life, you will understand. But I can assure you, little one, that I have been the father of dozens, perhaps hundreds of children, and I do not pretend to find them all interesting. Granny Harris would have been so much happier if she had not pretended to like Jim and June. And, by all the Gods, so should we!

Now that I look back on those days, when my brother

and I lived with old Granny Harris, I realize how lucky we were, and what a good woman she was. Many of our kind lead perfectly contented lives in the company of such as Granny Harris. She fed us regularly. She staggered faithfully off to the shop and staggered back again with tins of perfectly edible, if predictable food. She talked to us, and petted us, and stroked us. Being called by silly names was a small price to pay for such a life.

After all, for most of the time, we were free to lead the lives that our kind have always wanted to live. How often my brother and I have raced each other up and down the back walls of those terraced houses, biffed each other by the dustbins, or chased cabbage white about the little scrubs of gardens which sprouted in patches in Granny Harris's street. And then, with a delicious drowsiness coming over our limbs, we have trod the wall-top to the roof of her old shed and lain there, basking in the sunshine, and sinking into that warm delicious sleep which always has some of the qualities of the first warm sleep out of which we awoke to find ourselves being licked and purred into life by our beloved mother. Truly of all creatures, we cats have the greatest genius for *life*. I often thought it as we lay there meditating on the shed roof, and I have often thought it since. Dogs, silly fools, define all their existence in terms of the human race. They glory in their slavery. They whimper and yelp at their master's command. Human beings themselves have their moments of ingenuity. Keeping meat fresh in tins, for example, is a brilliant idea which only a human being would have thought of. But – poor silly creatures – how they scurry and fret. I watch them rushing hither and thither, taking on and off clothes, going to shops, driving their engines of murder, sitting in offices, and I wonder how many of them, for much of the time, share our acute consciousness simply of being *alive*. They are not so much themselves, as we are ourselves. They do not allow themselves the time to be fully human. We, by contrast, can give ourselves wholly and absolutely to being purely feline. And in those years with Granny Harris that was precisely what my brother and I did.

There were times of simple fun, such as I have described. There were times of great joy. Modesty forbids me to boast of the number of amorous conquests which I made in those years. Suffice it to say that I do not think there were many young lady cats in the neighbourhood who had not become acquainted with either my brother or myself. Serenading the pretty creatures by the rays of our Mother-of-Night, and fighting off rivals became our favourite nocturnal occupation.

I have been in so many bad fights since, that the scraps we got into during the Harris era now seem minor. The worst (or most humiliating) duel I ever had with one of our own kind during that period was while I was wooing a beautiful white Persian, who lived two or three streets away. My brother at the time was besotted with the tabby cat next door. When, one night on the shed roof, I said to him, "Do you smell what I smell?" he did not respond rationally.

"I only have nostrils for my darling!" he sighed.

"But do you?" I persisted. "That unmistakable smell is in the air. Somewhere, someone is waiting. I can feel it."

"You're welcome to her, old chap," he said. "Oh, I'm in love, I'm in love, brother. Do you think that she is thinking about me at this minute?"

I am sorry to say that I laughed at this question. My brother was a more sensitive soul than I. He really was in love. In those days – again, ah! how different I was then – the word love really meant nothing to me. As far as I was concerned, the world was full of beautiful female cats who were simply waiting for my attentions. But though I paid them court, and chased them and sang to them, I never allowed myself to be made unhappy by them.

So, I set off through the night, swishing my tail and following my nose, and feeling very sure both of myself and of my girl. The white Persian dame lived in a tall detached house and I had already made myself known to her. Even as

I approached the house, I let out a loud and highly musical cry of, "I'm coming, my own sweet."

"Are you indeed?" said a deep-throated male cat out of the darkness. "Well, along you come, and I'll give you what for."

Coming from a lighted street into the darkened garden, my sharp eyes were for a moment slow to see his, but then I saw them, gleaming bright green in the shadows.

"I think, Sir," I said with the pompous dignity of the very young — young males, at least, few females are pompous — "that you must be mistaken. I do not have the pleasure of your acquaintance..."

"'Op it," said the throaty voice.

"If you will excuse me," said I, "I am visiting a young lady who resides in this vicinity." And once again I started to sing. *I am coming, my own, my sweet.*

I could tell that my song excited considerable admiration, since in more than one house nearby, windows were being thrown open, curtains drawn back, and the stupid human audience were doing their best to appreciate it.

"Is that a cat?" I heard one ask. "I *think* it's only a cat."

"Sounded as though it was in pain."

Another voice was saying, "I thought for a nasty moment it was a woman being attacked." Another was shouting, "Belt up, can't you. Some of us are trying to sleep."

Poor coarse creatures, it was the best they could manage by way of musical appreciation. I have always rather prided myself on my singing voice. It was therefore particularly galling that a fellow cat should have come to share the human insensitivity on the point.

"You 'eard them," said the gravelly voice. "'Op it. This chick's mine."

I could by now hear my beautiful white Persian princess calling sweetly through the balmy night breeze.

"I'm coming, my own one!"

"No hurry!" I called back. "The joy of waiting is only

increased by the knowledge that you will soon be in my paws."

"Look mate," said gravelly voice. "Can you take an 'int or can't you?"

"You heard the lady," I said with some dignity. "Perhaps you can let her make up her own mind."

My rival came out into the moonlight. When I saw him my feelings of total contempt for him were mingled with sensations of pity. He was a very ill-favoured, rather over-weight ginger fellow. He was considerably older than I. In fact, he was so old that one could not help feeling that he was a bit past it.

"Wouldn't you be happier," I ventured, "curled up on a rug indoors?"

"What's that?" he asked, with the edginess of a cat who was about to become extremely angry. Curiously enough, I did not notice his rising wrath. I was so much looking forward to meeting my own, my white princess.

"Here I come, darling! I was doing my face!" she simpered through the shadows.

"It doesn't need doing," I called.

"Look, if you don't clear off, your face will be done over good and proper. With my claws," said the poor old ginger.

Well, it was understandable that an older, uglier cat should feel such jealousy of a younger and altogether more noble specimen. I also thought that he could be forgiven for being jealous of the tender way in which she called out, "Oh dear one, oh dear one!"

Poor old thing. Fat, jowly face, with bits dribbling from his mouth and eyes. The white parts of his fur rather grey. No effort had been made to keep himself looking nice, and he let off quite a pong. The idea that such a pathetic old wreck should still believe that he had any charms with the ladies was simply laughable.

You can imagine, then, how amazed I was when the white Persian princess came into sight. She scampered down a patch of lawn, looking more radiantly lovely in the moon-light than any cat I had ever seen. And then up some creeper and along a wall to the roof-top where I awaited her.

"Here I am!" she called ecstatically. "All yours, my dar-ling!"

And then she ran, quite firmly and quite deliberately, right up to the smelly old ginger tom and licked his face.

"I think," I said, as good-humouredly as I could manage, "that there has been some mistake..."

"Oh," said the beautiful white princess turning round, "it's *you*."

"Yes," I said with great self-satisfaction, "it is I, my own dear love."

The Princess lifted a soft paw and gently stroked the side of the ugly ginger's head.

"Darling," she said, in what I now began to see was a rather annoying, mincing tone of voice, "this silly little cat has been bothering me all week."

"Don't you worry, my darlin'," said ginger. "I'll soon sort '*im* out."

"Darling, would you? It would be so kind. He comes and bothers me all the time. And he wails these truly *frightful* songs!"

"Princess!" I exclaimed in dismay. "My own!"

But before the words were out of my mouth, old ginger had biffed me on the side of the head and almost knocked me off the shed roof.

"You!" I shouted. I couldn't think of what else to say. I just went on saying, "You, you, you!" Determined to have my revenge, I flung myself at old ginger, but he dodged me, and I went flying into the creeper.

It might have been possible to retrieve some dignity from this situation, even to pretend that I had meant to go and burrow among the leaves for some purpose, had it not been for Princess's high tinny laughter. (Had I ever thought high-ly of this silly piece of fluff? Surely not.)

"Now, mate. Got the 'int?" asked ginger rudely.

And Princess, nauseatingly, was cooing. "Oooh! You're so brave and strong," to the great oaf.

I was not going to stand for this. Throwing all caution to the winds, I flew at ginger's silly, smelly old face and managed to scratch him quite badly. But he was a skilled fighter, and I – at that stage – was not. The pain stung him into a perfectly timed riposte. Screaming with rage, we both clung to one another, biffing, scratching and shouting. The white princess, the bitch, stood by, encouraging the old fool to fight me. She was flattered to have two cats squabbling over her, and she was enjoying the contest as much as human beings enjoy watching that idiot electrical box with the coloured pictures on its screen.

Windows in houses were thrown wide open now, and human beings were adding their voices to our cries. "Shurrup!" "Blooming cats!" and so on.

I really did not deserve to win that fight. My footwork was clumsy, I was hitting all over the place. I had not thought out my tactics. But our great Mother-of-Night who shone down from the glowing summer sky was on my side. Ginger had winded me quite badly, and stung me with innumerable scratches. He was by now so furiously angry that he would, I think, have killed me if he could. And since he had reached this devastating stage of the contest, he instinctively stood back to admire his work, as we would stand back and look at a wounded mouse before moving in to the kill. And that was my moment of inspiration. I still had enough strength to lift a paw and punch him really hard in the face. And for the first time in that fight, I struck a blow which was properly aimed, and well-timed. He staggered from the blow and slipped. I think his feet were on some leaves on top of the shed roof. Anyhow, his hold slipped and he actually fell off the roof. Now at the bottom of the shed, there was a water butt. And I can tell you that there have been few more satisfying sounds to my ears than the sound of that fat old body sploshing into the barrel of cold water. Then, from the White Princess, what shrieks!

And after a little silence, what splutterings from ginger, "I'll get you! You — young — hooligan! I'll get you, if it is the last thing I do!"

But he never did get me. I did not stay to be got. And while he was shaking himself dry and saying he would get even with me, I sloped off through the shadows of the back gardens. My brother was not there in our own coal shed when I got home, I did not see him till the next morning when he was very sleepy.

"How did you get on last night?" he asked in the middle of a yawn.

"Oh, not so bad," said I.

CHAPTER SEVEN

One morning about mid summer, I woke up on my accustomed perch in the coal shed to see that it was fully daylight. I suppose I overslept because I had been on the prowl for most of the night, and taken refuge in the coal hole because I liked it there. I had already started to *prefer* sleeping outside human dwellings, instinct perhaps preparing me for the course that my life was going to take. Who can tell? My brother, poor thing, never really liked sleeping rough, as he called it, and preferred to be curled up in an armchair, or on the bed with one of these human beings. Of course, I have slept on beds where they have been sleeping, but it is a devil of a job. They disturb a cat with their infernal snoring and their tossing and turning, and their getting up in the middle of the night to sit on the well.

Anyway, I awoke on a glorious, bright day in June, to hear my brother's voice calling out to me. He sounded excited, but also distressed. Something was obviously up.

"What is it? I'm in here!" I called, through the hole in the coal shed wall.

"Come out! Come at once. Something's happened!" he called.

"*What*'s happened?" I asked.

I crawled through the side of the shed, on to the roof, and down into the little yard, taking care to avoid the rattling dustbin lid which woke the neighbours, and called down on my head one night not merely cursings and imprecations, but also a bucket of cold water.

"Come and see," said my brother.

"Don't be mysterious," said I. "If something's happened, tell me."

"I can't tell," he said. "That's why I want you to see. Come on."

He looked both excited and frightened. It was a look which sometimes came into his face before a fight. Then he turned and trotted towards the back door and through the cat-flap. I followed him, through the kitchen and up the narrow staircase, towards Granny's bedroom.

"It's in here," he said.

"What is?"

"Well, it's sort of *her*, and yet it isn't her. You'll see what I mean. What do you make of it?"

He jumped on to Granny's bed, and I followed him, purring automatically as I always did when jumping up to greet her, and kneading the bedding with my claws. I could not imagine what my brother was making such a fuss about, or why he was referring to Granny's sleeping body as "it" rather than "her". But then I saw.

For a start, its eyes were still open, and yet they were no longer the eyes of Granny Harris. And for another thing, she was motionless. Quite still. There was no breath in her, no motion, and no colour. She lay there as stiff as a board.

"What do you think?" he asked.

I did not *think* anything. I knew that the best human friend I was ever going to have had been taken away from me, and that this *thing* had been left in her place. It was a mockery of her, and of us. It did not even look particularly like her. By now, in the normal course of things, Granny would have been calling out, "Good morning, my darling," and sitting up against her pillows, and stroking us. And after a bit of play, she would say, "Can't stay in bed all day," and she would heave herself off the side of the bed, and waddle off to sit on the well. And then she would go to the kitchen, and give us some food, and boil up the kettle to make herself some tea, and we would all go back to the bedroom and sit on the bed while the box of voices spoke. But today the box of voices was silent, just as Granny was silent, and although neither my brother nor I knew what had happened, we both knew that our lives had for ever changed.

Since – oh since! How many times, too many times, have I seen this silence, this stillness, this stiffness, this nothingness come upon living creatures, creatures, very often whom I have loved? And you will see it too. And no more than I, will you be able to understand it or know what it is, but it is the great enemy, which we all resist, even though we know from experience that there are worse enemies, like pain and degradation and disease.

"I'm hungry," said my brother.

"Me too," said I.

But I was still staring with fascination at the thing. I went right up to its face and touched it with my paw, unable to believe the change which had taken place during the night.

"Is there any food which we can get at in the kitchen?" asked my brother.

"Let's go and look."

In the larder, there were the remains of an old chicken carcass, which we took from the shelf. I am afraid we smashed the plate as we did so, but who was there now to mind? (Little did we guess!) There was not much meat on the bird, and we ate what there was in no time. There was probably milk kept shut in the cold white house, but neither of us could open it, nor get at the bottles there, any more than we could open the closed tins of meat with which Granny Harris would normally have fed us.

Your time-scale as a young cat is very short: as mine was. You don't think more than a few hours ahead. This is a good thing in one way – it stops you worrying. But in other ways, it makes life much *more* agitating. Now, if I were in that position today, with Granny lying silent and stiff upstairs, I would know that something, sometime would happen. Someone would bring food, or I could go out and find food somewhere else. Something would happen. But neither my brother nor I could understand this. Now that the situation had changed, we assumed that it had changed for ever.

And that house, which had been such a very good home to us, for about two years, had suddenly become a place of nightmare. It was like a cruel practical joke. We knew that there was food to be found, but we could not get at it. It was all locked up – in the cold white house, in tins, in cupboards. And we did not even try to see that the situation would not be like this forever. Such a thought was beyond us. When we had finished the chicken, we were still ravenously hungry, and it made us panic. We raced around the house, knocking things everywhere. A lamp went and was smashed to pieces on the parlour floor. Cups flew off the kitchen dresser. And the bedroom table in the room where it lay was soon reduced to a chaos. The necklaces and brooches and little pots of cream which stood there were all sent flying.

We did not know what we were doing. We were in a sort of mad state. I've been in it since on a number of occasions. If you've ever been like it, you'll know what I mean. You don't *think*. You don't want to destroy things, though destroy things you certainly do. You just want to run round and round and get rid of the excitement, the devilry, whatever it is, by hyperactivity. It happens to me less now than it did, thanks be to our Mother-of-Night.

After about an hour of it, my brother said, "This is no use. We'll have to go and hunt."

"We'll starve else," said I.

It wasn't a bad morning's hunt. At the bottom of the yard there was a family of mice, and I got two of them. My brother got a pigeon from a nearby garage roof, which he was kind enough to share with me. In all our many hunting expeditions together, we never fought over food. The pigeon was delicious, moist, warm and red: the only way to eat a bird, in my view. How your human can cook it in an oven and even cover it with pastry (!) is beyond me.

The advantage of our short-sightedness (in time terms) is that my brother and I had decided immediately that this was the way we were going to live for the rest of our lives; and

so we did not keep returning to the house expecting someone to open tins for us. We caught, or stole, our next three
or four meals. This was just as well, because Granny Harris
was all alone in that house, getting stiffer and paler and
(I fear) smellier, for four whole days. I suppose that if she
had been one of those people who are visited each day
by a milkman, this would not have been so. But she only
had milk delivered twice a week, and anything she needed
beyond this was collected from the corner shop. It was the
milkman who discovered her. And the funny thing is, that
when my brother and I realized that we were not the only
ones to know about Granny, we felt guilty.

"That's torn it now," I said.

"I reckon we should hide," said my brother.

And hide we did from the moment that the milkman came
round the back of the house and said there was something
up because Granny had not answered the door or left her
milk money.

From the shed at the end of the garden we watched the
whole sorry business. We watched the milkman ringing and
ringing. Then we heard him call Granny's name through the
letter box. He went back to his van and talked to a neighbour. Then, the two of them came and tried to force open
the kitchen window. They failed. Then they smashed it and
opened it, and one of them climbed in.

"As we feared," said one, coming to open the door for the
other.

And then, there was the ambulance and a police car, and
they came to carry what had been Granny away in a sort of
black bag, and the window was boarded up, and the doors
locked, and the house made fast, and we were left alone.
That took all day somehow, and it was only at nightfall that
we began to feel we had the place to ourselves.

After a light evening supper (we had burst into a kitchen
some doors up and stolen the Whiskas from the plate of a
pampered little kitten owned by a young architect and his
wife, and rounded it off with a sparrow from the architect's

garden) we had returned to Granny's kitchen and were discussing what to do next.

"I reckon we're safer in the house," I said.

"Unless other people come to live in the house," said my brother.

"Are they likely to do that?"

"I don't know."

"If they did, would we stay?"

"You seem to think I know all the answers to all the questions," laughed my brother. "I ask you questions I don't know the answer to myself. It's just a way of thinking aloud. I reckon we are a damn sight better off here than we would be somewhere else. We know our territory. We are warm and comfortable. With a bit more practice, we'll be able to feed ourselves properly, by hunting or scavenging."

"There's the whole area of dustbins," I said, "which remains relatively unexplored."

"And meanwhile," said my brother, "we have the whole house to ourselves."

"Don't speak too soon," said I.

"What's that?"

We were in the back kitchen. Suddenly we both stood stock still. We could hear the front door being opened and the voices of June and Jim, quarrelling as usual.

"How d' you expect me to remember the cats on top of everything else?" Jim was saying.

"It was you who egged her on to buy the things."

"Me? It was you and our Tracy..."

Jabber, jabber, jabber, jabber, jabber.

When Granny was still with us, we would often, all three of us, have a bit of a laugh about June and Jim and their jabbering voices, their endless quarrelling, their gracelessness. Granny was always too nice to say that she was glad they did not call very often, but she always seemed peaceful and happier when they had gone.

"If you looked after your mother properly it would never have happened."

"I like that! It was you who was the one..."

"Let's scarper," said my brother.

We got out through the cat-flap and, by the back door, we sat and listened.

"Jim."

"What is it now?"

"Did you hear that?"

"Hear what?"

"Jim, you don't think there's burglars, do you? You know when someone's passed away, they often..."

"Don't talk daft. What's there to steal? It'll be one of the cats in the back kitchen, you go and see."

"Jim, I don't want to go and see."

"Don't be so daft. There's nothing'll hurt you there. Go on, woman."

"You go, Jim."

"I'm looking here. You go in the back."

"You're as scared as I am, Jim Harbottle."

"I'm not scared."

"You are..."

And so on.

It would be tedious to rehearse the oafish manner in which the Harbottles set about finding and catching us. You do not want to read about them stumbling out into the backyard and debating whose fault it was that Jim had stood on a rake, whose handle bounced up and hit him on the head. No more do you want to read about June colliding with the dustbin and subsequently explaining that she would never have done so if Jim would just be that bit more careful; nor of Jim saying, for some reason, that he "liked that". Having failed to see us looking down at them from the roof of the shed, they returned to the house and looked for a torch, and then back to the car, where they found one, and then more banging and searching, and whistling and calling. I suppose that we should have been flattered. Probably, by then, however, they had long since ceased to care about whether they found us. The search had become a competition, and the reason that neither would abandon it was they felt certain that when one found me, the other would be made to look a fool. I did not realize this at the time, not knowing June and Jim well. It was mere whim, that after about half an hour of watching them crash about in the dark, I said to my brother, "They'd probably be able to open a tin for us."

"Shall we go and put them out of their misery?" he asked.

"I can't bear much more of this noise," I said.

And so, we ran to greet Jim and June. How different things would be if we had not done that! Sometimes, late at night, I pace about in the dark among the back gardens of the street where you live, little Grandkitten. And I think of that moment in my life. I hear a human voice calling out into the darkness. "Puss, puss, puss!" Probably in most cases, nothing turns on whether or not a cat heeds the call. But if, on that occasion, we had stayed where we were in the safety of the dark, our lives might have been much happier. And, who knows, my brother might be alive today. It is only because we do not know what fortune holds in store for us that we are able to act at all. Quite unconscious of the significance of our actions, we ran towards Jim and June with no more serious thought in our heads than the idea that Jim might open us a tin of meat.

"See," said June, as we approached. "I told you whistling was no good."

"What d' you mean, no good. They've come, haven't they?"

"When I called, they came."

"I like that! It was my whistle that did it."

This ding-dong quarrel, in which Jim was always trying to get the better of June, and June was always claiming that she *had* got the better of Jim, went on, as far as we were concerned, for the next year or so. For Jim and June, having taken us into Granny's kitchen and fed us with some tinned food, bundled us into a blanket, and took us home to live with them.

CHAPTER EIGHT

Jim and June had a much bigger, more "comfortable" house than Granny Harris. "Comfortable", I mean, by the standards of the human race. We both found it unpleasantly hot, particularly in the winter months when there were radiators on in every room. Each window had not one, but two panes of glass. If you were in Granny Harris's kitchen and you wanted to go out into the yard, she would just open the window and let you out. But in Jim and June's kitchen, you could not open the window. Granny Harris washed her few dishes by dipping them in hot soapy water in her sink. But June and Jim washed their dishes by putting them in a cupboard which roared and churned and shuddered. It was a horrible noise.

The noise was one of the worst things about that house. It never seemed to stop, and there was not a room in the house where some noise was not going on. When Jim and June sat on the well, they switched on a whirring electric fan. When they were in bed, they played the box of voices continually. Downstairs in the room they called the lounge, there was a coloured screen showing a constant display of idiot human behaviour: men kicking balls into nets (Jim loved this). Men driving engines of murder. Women with their arms in soap suds which they said were as soft as their faces. And with the pictures, a constant stream of noise. In Tracy's bedroom upstairs, which had a strangely sweet smell that somehow got up your nose, the box of voices, quite a small one, played loud pulsating music which scared us silly. While she listened to it, Tracy (whom we quite liked) would bob up and down and dance in rhythm to the horrible noises.

And in addition to all these artificial noises, the people

made noises with their mouths all day long. They were of very uncertain temper. You could never be sure whether they were going to be all cooing and soppy, or unaccountably angry. They seemed to be cross with each other most of the time. If Jim went out to the side of the house on a Sunday morning to polish the engine of murder, June would come and rail at him for not having put up some shelves in the spare room. If Jim was getting dressed in the morning, he seemed unable to do so without opening the warm cupboard in the room where they washed, and shouting that he could not see any socks or shirts or pants. I do not understand this business of clothes and the importance they attach to them; but I must say they look very peculiar without them – hardly any fur at all, except in scrubs and patches. Just extensions of pink bare flesh like a poor creature that has been half-skinned.

I have mentioned the noise. But the worst thing of all was the simple fact that we were prisoners there. There was no cat-flap in the back door. On some evenings, June was the aggressor.

"When are you going to put a cat-flap in the door?" she would ask. "Honestly, Jim Harbottle, you are the laziest —"

"I'm tired. I've had a very tiring day at the office. I —"

"Tired! You're lazy. And you drink too much. That's your second can of beer. I've been watching you."

On other evenings Jim took the initiative.

"I've just been talking to Mr Jones down the road," he said with a confident smile. "He says that ever since they put in that cat-flap they've had all the strays in the neighbourhood coming into their kitchen. See!"

"See what?"

"See why I don't like your idea of a cat-flap?"

"It wasn't my idea. It was your idea to put one in mum's house."

"She was getting elderly. She couldn't get up and let cats out every time they wanted to go..."

This was the trouble. We could not come and go as we

pleased. We were prisoners, and entirely subservient to Jim and June's trivial routines and whims. At first, I thought that the frustration might actually kill my brother. For the first few times when we were shut up in June's kitchen with all its whirring machinery, he paced up and down all night, cursing her and her stupid ways. He was still very much missing his girlfriend whom we had been forced to abandon when we left Granny Harris's house. Poor chap. I did not know what he was suffering then, because I did not yet understand what it was to suffer from a great love. I tried to laugh him out of it, and to imply that there were other fish in the sea.

"But not in this kitchen," he observed drily. "And when were we last fed?"

That was another thing. June usually fed us, but she did not always remember to do so. And when she forgot, she would say that it was not always her job to feed us, and why didn't Jim take his turn at feeding us for a change. Sometimes we would go for twenty-four hours without being fed properly. It was just as well that Jim had told us about the cat-flap down the road at Mrs Jones. Often when we ignominiously went to tell June that we "wanted to go out" (How would you feel if you had to announce each time your bladder needed emptying?) we would scamper off to Mrs Jones's house. I sometimes feel twinges of guilt about the dear old cat who lived there. Mrs Jones would put out some delicious meals for him: mashed tuna, chopped fresh lights, heart or liver. He was a spoilt old thing whom she called Major. He was a stately black cat full of years.

"Major! Major!" she would call. "Dindins, Major!"

Quick as a flash, we would go through the cat-door, wolf the delectable meal which she had put down for him, and run out into his garden. It was there, I remember, that I really developed my taste for lights. Then you would hear Mrs Jones's voice again.

"I don't know what you are mewing for, after that *lovely* dindins. No, no. You'll get fat if I give you any more."

And poor old Major would come toddling out to talk to us in the garden.

"Old woman's getting forgetful. Thinks she's fed me when she hasn't. Not that I mind. You eat less as you get older. Sometimes, she gives me these great big helpings and I can hardly start them. At least she keeps off the tinned muck."

"Ours doesn't," said my brother. "It's nothing but tinned muck – *when* she remembers."

"No, she does me very well," said the Major with a yawn. "Couldn't do with tinned muck."

"Does she play the box of voices all the time, like ours?" asked my brother.

"The dear old Beeb?" asked the Major, bafflingly. He always called the box of voices the Beeb, for some reason which I do not to this day understand. "I expect she does. To tell the truth, old boy, I'm getting just a bit deaf, so I don't always notice. Wouldn't mind if she did. It's children I can't stand."

"There are no young children in our house," I said.

"Oh, are there?" said the Major. "Bad luck." But as soon as he had said this, he fell asleep.

For ever afterwards, the Major had it in his head that we lived in a house infested with young children. If you passed him on a garden wall, he would murmur, "Good day to ye. How are those damned kids?" And any advice you might want to ask him, as an older and wiser cat, would always be given from the viewpoint that we had a lot of kids to contend with.

One morning, after we had just stolen a particularly generous helping of mashed tuna from the Major's dish (Mrs Jones: "I mashed it up nicely to help you to chew, so I don't know what you are mewing about."), we sat with him on the teak bench by his minder's rose garden and asked his advice about the budgerigar.

"They got it for the kids, I expect," he said.

"No," I said. "It belonged to Granny Harris originally.

Then they took it because Granny was afraid we would kill it. But as it turned out, we are sharing a house with the wretched thing after all."

"It really annoys me," said my brother.

"Don't blame you," said the Major. "I'd be annoyed if I had to share a house with a lot of kids. Enough to make a chap take to the road."

It was on the Major's lips that I first heard this expression, "take to the road", and from the beginning it had romance for me. It is a curious fact that my brother and I both *stayed* with Jim and June. Neither of us liked it there. Instinct, you would have thought, would have made us set off. But it was only when I heard the phrase "take to the road" that the full possibility of escape occurred to me. Oh, I had been corrupted by my years as the "pet" of Granny Harris. I had begun to believe that human beings were necessary to my existence. I had begun to regard Jim and June (only begun, mind) as essential to my survival. Where else would the food come from? The answer, as my brain and eyes told me, was all around. But that was not how it *felt* at the time. But sometimes a single word is enough to change our lives. Something, even as the Major said, "take to the road", stirred within me. I knew that it described my own predicament and adventure; the destiny I was to follow. But it was just a casual remark in the middle of our conversation about the budgerigar.

"It twitters at you all the time," said my brother. "I shouldn't think it would taste very good, but sometimes I'd just like to sink my teeth in it to shut it up."

"I bit a kid once," said the Major. "Let off one hell of a hullabaloo, yelling and wailing the way they do."

"It isn't a kid," I said loudly. "It's a budgerigar."

"No need to shout, old boy. Budgerigars are a different matter. Silly little fellas." He smiled almost tolerantly. "Did I ever tell you the story of how I once chased a parrot?"

He had often told us the story of how he chased the parrot. It had got out of its cage and the Major had chased it to the top of a cupboard. Then a person had come into the room, and caught the parrot and put it back into its cage. It was not exactly an interesting story.

"You see," said the Major, warming to his theme, "the stupid creature had got out of its cage..."

"Jim would be furious if you killed the budgie," I said.

"Jim is furious anyway," said my brother.

"So is June," I said. "Well, nice talking to you, Major, we must be off."

"Don't you want to hear the end of the story, old boy? You see," he laughed to himself, "it had flown up to the top of this cupboard..."

He was still telling the story to himself when we got up to go.

For most of that day – although it was a beautiful, hot sunny day, when we could have been sunning ourselves in the garden – we were cooped up in the house. Jim took his little briefcase from the hall and went out to work. June went round the house with the annoying roaring-machine which she rubbed up and down on the carpets. The only good thing about this particular bit of machinery was that it had a long string-affair attached to the hole in the wall and if you were bored stiff (as we were for most of the time) it made a good game to "hunt the machine" as it roared over the rugs and floor, and to chase the string affair as if it were a snake.

It was no substitute for the Hunt, but there was a certain degree of simple pleasure to be derived from stalking the roaring-machine and pulling at its snake. My brother and I took it in turns to yank the snake or prowl after the machine.

"Can't you play elsewhere?" was cross June's comment on our sport. "How can I hoover with you two under my feet all the while? I could murder that Jim for bringing you back here. You've been nothing but trouble ever since you came."

Sometimes, as she pushed the machine about the house, she would chunter for as long as half an hour about how angry she was with us, angry with Jim, angry with Tracy, angry with just about everyone. It is a curious fact, but you seldom meet a human being who exactly likes another human being. They do not mix well. In this, I am told, they resemble the moles.

Anyway, on this occasion, June shut us out of the bedroom where we were so happily playing, and we went downstairs to the lounge to talk to and about the budgie.

My brother was quite right. It was, in truth, a dreary little bird. It sat for most of the day on a perch, staring at itself in a tiny circular looking-glass. Sometimes it ate seed, and sometimes, when the seed had nourished it, the inevitable waste product came out at the other end and dropped on to the floor of its cage. Otherwise it made the occasional flap flap, tweet tweet. Probably the sensible thing to do would have been to ignore it, but I couldn't, and nor could my brother. We were fascinated by schemes of how we might get it out of its cage and tear the boring little thing limb from limb.

"Just look at it," said my brother. "Sitting there."

"They spend a good deal more time looking at that budgie than they do at us," I said.

"Naturally," said my brother with sarcasm. "Do you think that if we jumped hard enough, we could knock the cage off its shelf?"

"That would be fun," I said. "But could we get the thing out of its cage if we did so?"

We jumped up to the shelf where the cage was located, and made very savage faces at the little thing. I have heard tell of cats frightening small birds to death. Not much sport in that, I should have thought. No, to get any pleasure out of a bird, there must be a chase. And my brother and I both realized there would be no particular fun in just getting the wretched budgie out of its cage.

The people, by the way, called the budgerigar Henry, and it was a fashion of address which we, as a mark of disrespect, took to adopting.

"Henry, Henry, Henry," we squeaked mockingly, pawing the cage.

How he squeaked back! Doubtless in his own silly language he was saying that we were bullies and cads.

"They think they love him," said my brother. "But what a strange way of showing your love to a fellow creature, by locking him up in a cage. Now I imagine that a budgerigar, however awful we may find poor Henry, would really be better off leading its tedious existence in a tree."

We jumped down from the shelf and settled ourselves in a snug spot behind the sofa, where the sun shone down very hotly and where it was a delight to sit, particularly since someone had drawn back the double-glazing and opened a window so that the warm air which fell upon us was fresh and natural, wholly unlike the heat of a radiator.

"I believe," said I, "that budgerigars come from far, far away." And with these words, "far far away", in my mind I must have drifted off into a deep sleep. I was thinking, too, of the Major's words, "take to the road", and I think perhaps in that deep sleep of mine I first began to dream of a free life and a roving life, in which we depended upon no human master, no bondage or centrally-heated prison house. Did I say that I *first* began to dream? What nonsense! This dream had been with me from the beginning. It was the dream from which I awoke in my mother's paws. But from that day, it was one which began to focus. In my dreams I began to visualize an actual road, a straight road, moonlit and leading across flat country. At the end of it there was some blessed goal which I could not discern, but the approach made my heart ache not with weariness or oppression, but a sort of joy. I cannot really describe it. It was a feeling that the further out of my way I seemed to go, the closer I was drawing to my home.

Very different thoughts were forced upon us when we

woke. The sleep must have been deep indeed, because much appeared to have transpired during our time of dreaming. Outside the window there was an enormous red engine of murder, to which had been attached a huge ladder and a coil of hose pipes. It was being manned by a group of curious creatures who were half-snail, half-human. That is, although they had human bodies, their heads were encased not in fur but in hard shells, bright yellow in colour. There was a lot of shouting going on. A crowd of people had assembled in the garden. June stood in the midst of them wailing and chewing a handkerchief.

"Dear little Henry," she kept saying. "He's such a friend-ly little budgie!"

Jumping onto the back of the sofa and looking out of the open lounge window, we could survey the scene from a better vantage point. The ladder from the red engine had a sort of basket or crow's nest at the top of it. It was directed to a telegraph wire in the Harbottle's garden. One of the yellow-shells was standing in the crow's nest, while on the wire, hopping from foot to foot and twittering with excite-ment, was Henry.

Down below June was still crying.

"I didn't know that the window was open. I just let him out of his cage for a little fly around the room and he . . . he . . ." It was too much for her. Tears made it impossible to finish the sentence.

"He flew up there. Look!" said a neighbour.

"And to think!" murmured my brother to me. "He was flying round this room while we sat behind the sofa asleep! We'll never have such an opportunity again."

The thought made us doubly angry with Henry.

The yellow-shelled man in the crow's nest was being moved by the men below so that he was almost within reach of Henry. An inch nearer . . . and another inch, and he could merely stretch out and grab the little budgerigar in his paw. But just as yellow-shell reached out to grab Henry, the little bird flapped its wings and flew! First it settled on top of a telegraph pole. The crowd below gasped, as if the whole episode were being put on for their entertainment. The yellow-shells shouted to one another, and the sort of ladder-affair was moved, with the man still in it at the top, so that it was quite near the spot where Henry was perched. But then Henry flew off a second time, and this time he settled in the branches of a tree.

It is a curious fact to record. When he was locked up in his cage tweeting at us in the house, my brother and I felt nothing but contempt for Henry. But when we saw the crowd of people, and the oafish yellow-shells all trying to catch one little bird, our sympathies shifted. We longed for him to be able to escape, to fly far far away, to escape and do the budgie equivalent of taking to the road. At last, he was a free creature. And the crowd who were all staring at him, and oo-ing and ah-ing every time he flew away had no claim upon him.

Go little bird! Be free!

These, truly, were the sentiments of both of us. And I record them because some people might not believe them in the light of what happened subsequently.

While Henry was lost among the boughs of the leafy sycamore, Jim Harbottle returned, carrying his little case, as he did each evening around six o'clock. He looked considerably alarmed by the sight of the red engines parked outside his house, and by all the people, and by June crying, and by the yellow-shells.

"Jim Harbottle, Gas Board," he said, shaking the paw of one of the yellow-shells.

"Good evening, but we don't need the gas board," said the yellow-shell. And then a surprising thing happened. Yellow-shell took off his shell and underneath you saw that he was just another man in uniform.

"No," said Jim, "I work for the Gas Board. Regional Area Manager."

"I believe you," said the man in uniform. "But we don't need the Gas Board."

"I assure you," said Jim with some dignity, "that you do.

70

Without the Gas Board, where would this country – I might even ask, this *world* – be? Gas is a dangerous source of energy unless used efficiently, and effectively, and safely. That is why you need the Gas Board. That is why the Gas Board needs Area Managers. Without them, there would be explosions and calamities all over —"

"Yes, yes," said the man in uniform. "But there's no gas leak."

"And no fire?" asked Jim.

"No fire."

"Forgive me," said Jim, "but when the Area Manager of the Gas Board returns home and sees fire engines parked outside his house, he not unnaturally assumes that there has been a fire or ... a gas leak."

And then June came forward sniffing and crying. "Oh, Jim, he's up the tree!"

"What is? A cat?" asked Jim. "You called the fire brigade at great expense to the local rate payer just because a cat is up a tree? Let it stay there!"

"Never really took to cats," he told the fireman. "Dogs, yes, I am a dog man. But not cats. We only took these two cats out of the kindness of our hearts after my mother-in-law passed away."

"Really, sir?"

"He'd never have got out if you hadn't left the window open in the lounge," said June.

"Me? I like that! Me leave a window open?"

"You can't deny it, Jim Harbottle. It was not me who opened the window of the lounge."

"It gets stuffy in there. Anyway, even if I did, it's hardly my fault if a cat goes up a tree."

"It isn't a cat up the tree," said June. "It's Henry. Our beautiful budgie..." And at this she began to cry again.

Evidently Jim, who had never really taken to the likes of us, was very devoted to budgies, or perhaps simply, any stick, even the twig on which Henry was perched, was good enough to beat his wife with.

"You let the budgie out!"

71

"There's no need to take that tone with me, Jim Harbottle!"

"You opened the budgie's cage and let it out and then you have the cheek to tell *me* that I left a window open."

"The bird still seems to be in the tree, sir," said the fireman, looking up towards Henry who was free and happy in the branches.

"Ah, yes," said Jim importantly. "So he is. It is very kind of you — er, officer — to have put the resources of the Fire Service at our disposal on this particular occasion."

"It's hard to see what we can do, sir, really," said the fireman. "If the budgie wants to be up in the tree, there is not very much we can do about it."

Jim looked at him with the look of a man who believed that the Gas Board would have been able to do something, even if the Fire Brigade were to fail.

So eventually, the ladder was lowered, and the men (they were all men, it turned out) got into the fire engines, and they drove away, and the crowd dispersed. All that evening, Jim and June quarrelled and railed at each other, while they switched on and off the various machines in their house. Tracy returned for supper, to find her parents standing in the garden trying to lure Henry down from the tree with a dish of seeds. But he wouldn't come. After the meal, Tracy said she was going out with her friend Bob, and she left her parents to their wrangling.

They were much too busy quarrelling to think of feeding *us*. By the time darkness fell, we were both ravenous, but when we went into the lounge to drop a gentle hint, to the effect that a little supper would be most welcome, Jim shouted rudely, "Oh stop your caterwauling," and hit me really very hard on the nose with a rolled-up newspaper. I cursed him, and went to claw the floor by the back door, hoping at least that I might be let out. My brother came too, and eventually, June remembered that we had not, as she put it, "spent a penny", and let us out into the darkness of the night. I scampered down to the Major's house. In his kitchen the old boy was snoozing by the warm Aga. Under the sink was a bowl of chicken breasts which he had hardly touched. I made short work of that before Mrs Jones came in and shooed me out, shouting, "Go back and eat your own food. Honestly, those Harbottle cats seem permanently hungry."

For my nightly lavatory activities, I managed to find a neat little patch among Jim's favourite petunias, and then I scampered in through the back door where June was calling, "Come on puss, puss, puss."

There was no harm in June, she was just an idiot. The same could not be said for Jim. I think he was rather enjoying her distress at the loss of the budgie.

"No point in shouting for Henry," he called.

"I was just getting the cats in. More than you ever do."

"I should think that budgie's done for," said Jim. "What a stupid thing to do, to let it out of its cage."

"Here comes Bootsie!" said June, trying to rise above Jim's taunts.

And from the shadows of the garden, my brother came running. He was carrying something in his jaws, something bright green, feathery, and lifeless.

"Now what have you got there?" asked June.

And when the thing was dropped at her feet, she let out a squeal of horror and grief. My brother looked at me, and licked his lips with a little bit of embarrassment. "Just couldn't resist," he murmured.

CHAPTER NINE

Things were never quite the same again after my brother had killed Henry. Jim and June, who were opposed to one another in all areas of life, became united in their loathing of us. The feeding became even less regular, and the outbursts of rage against us now came from both of them. I got used to avoiding Jim's foot. If he passed me in the hall or on the landing, he would kick me. June was little better, and often, when putting down a bowl of food for us, would smack us on the back of the head when we began to eat. Our only ally in the household was Tracy, and soon she left to live with her boyfriend Bob. Jim made a tremendous fuss about this, but I could not blame Tracy. When he was not being rude to his wife or attacking us, he was forever shouting at the girl because he did not like her hair, or her clothes, or the way she had decorated her room. No wonder she left, but when she left, she left us to their mercy. One day, while we were hiding from them under the bed in Tracy's room – now, so still and quiet – my brother said calmly, "I'm not sure that I can endure this for very much longer."

"Nor can I."

"It seems so pointless to be living like this," he said. "Do you know why I killed that budgerigar? I did not realize it at the time. But looking back, I see that it is months since you and I got any decent hunting."

"It is months since we just led a normal feline existence, not constantly bothered by that pair," I said.

"Have you heard the latest?" asked my brother.

"No."

"Jim's talking about getting a dog. Alsatian. June asked

him how he thinks an Alsatian would get on with us and he said, 'I wouldn't mind if it bit their heads off.' He's not a very nice man, isn't Jim."

"We couldn't live here with a dog," I said.

"What I can't make out is why Jim and June want one. A dog will be much more 'trouble' than we are. A dog is dangerous. A dog has no control over its bladder or bowels. They'll have to spend months training it not to make messes in the lounge. And yet this is what they want. Really..."

"They are extraordinary."

We said it in chorus, and the old catch-phrase brought a little comfort. After we had sat together in silence for a little space, I said, "Are you serious about getting away?"

"Almost enough to make a cat take to the road," said my brother in his (quite good) imitation of the Major's voice.

"So that phrase stuck with you, too?"

"Oh, brother," he said, "wouldn't it be nice to rove the world and simply be ourselves; to eat when we wanted, and how we wanted. On warm nights, to be out, hunting or lovemaking. To be free!"

If only we had acted on impulse! If only, then and there, we had decided to run away from Jim and June and to take to the road. But my brother was a cautious cat, who believed where possible in planning any big course of action. He took to having long conversations with the Major about our plans, and the Major insisted upon the importance of reconnaissance.

"Must have a recce," said the old cat, warming to his theme. "Most important. Now when I was a young cat, I used to know the whole of this area; not just to the end of the road, but far beyond. My advice to you both is to head out in that direction. Follow the path across the open field and you will come to the banks of a river. Always a good spot for immediate food supplies. If you're lucky you'll get a duck. There will be water-rats, field mice..."

But the next day, after a bit of recce, my brother returned. The Major's open field was now covered with houses.

"Of course. Not been there for some time, old boy. Don't get about as often as I did."

Nevertheless, he had persuaded us of one important idea and that was, for the first few weeks of our life on the road, we should try to avoid human beings as much as possible, and their houses and roads. He told us – what I now know to be true – that when you go on the road, there is a danger of being pursued. They will put up advertisements in local shop windows, and ring up the police and the yellow-shells. There were other dangers on the road, too, about which the Major was vague. I know them better now! But I still think if we had only set out then, together, all might have been well. A day never passes in my solitude without my thinking of my brother, or missing his companionship. But almost more than his loss, I regret the manner of his loss. It makes me so very angry. It was all such a waste of life and opportunity.

My brother was always much more inclined than I was (at that period) to keep his ear to the ground, and to be aware of what the human beings were intending. It was he who got wind of the fact that Jim and June were going away to another town called Spain, which they had read about in one of the pieces of paper which I had scratched with my claws. It was a hot place, and Jim and June had the ambition to change their poor furless flesh from the colour of uncooked sausages to the colour of dog-messes. My brother said that it was going to cost them a considerable amount of money to do this. How he knew, I do not know. Once it became more or less certain that they were indeed going away (and once he explained it all to me, I remembered that they had been away the previous year to bathe – if you please – in grease, as if there wasn't enough of it in the bottles on June's bedroom table) our plans began to be formed. We would allow them to go away, and hope that they would do so having forgotten to shut us up in the house. If not, we would have to escape from the house on the first occasion when someone came in to feed us. Then we would run three or four streets away, keeping only to back gardens and avoiding main roads, and find our way into some sort of park which my brother had discovered on his recces. It makes me sad to talk of the plans now. What actually happened was so pathetically different.

June and Jim set off for Spain all right.

Getting their things packed in a suitcase, getting the suitcase down the stairs, running up and down stairs in search of a lost passport which was not lost at all, just in Jim's other jacket, debating whether it was June's fault or Jim's that the passport was in this jacket, and whose fault it had been on that holiday, three years ago, when they had left without their travellers' cheques, took quite a bit of time.

"Have you locked the back door?"

"Course."

"Put out food for Bootsie and Fluffie?"

"You said *you'd* do that."

"Oh, you are *hopeless*."

It was while she was spooning some muck into a saucer for us that the front doorbell rang, and a man said he was a taxi.

"Goodbye, Bootsie! Goodbye, Fluffie!" called June in a very silly voice indeed.

"Come on, d' you want us to miss the aeroplane?" Jim was asking her.

"I do hope Tracy and Bob remember to feed the cats."

"Well, they will if you remembered to tell them."

"Course I remembered. More than you have ever done. Honestly, Jim, I've had to do everything: cancel the milk, cancel the bread, ring up the police to tell them we're going away."

"Everything except pay for the holiday," said Jim.

Their querulous voices echoed down the path. That was the last time we ever heard them. I do not miss them much. You, who have a kinder view of the human race than I do, will think that I have given an unfair picture of June and Jim, but I do not think so.

They left us behind, locked up in their house. There was no window, no cat-flap in the back door, and the litter-tray which we might have used as a lavatory was in the kitchen. The only trouble was that they had shut the kitchen door, so there was no way of getting to it. We were therefore "at large" in the house, and it was inevitable, after what felt like countless hours, that we should have used the sitting-room as a lavatory. I wish I could pretend that it gave me no satisfaction to have "used" the two-seater settee in front of their coloured picture box. My brother, more discreetly, "went" upstairs – in the bath to be precise.

The hours when we were locked up in that house felt very long. They *were* very long. We were shut up, in fact, with nothing to eat, and nowhere appropriate to go to the lavatory for the whole of that day, and, almost, for the whole of the next. Tracy and her boyfriend were meant to have come in and fed us "at regular intervals", but there was no sign of them until the following evening. We heard the front door being opened, and Bob, Tracy's boy, saying, "Cor what a stink!"

"Oh don't," she said, "I think I'll be sick."

They came into the house holding their noses. Then Tracy, whom I had thought of as a friend called out, "Bootsie! Fluffie! Come on, then!"

I ran to her purring and nuzzled against the fishnet stockings which she wore on her legs.

"Oh Fluffie, what have you done?" she said.

"You can smell what he's done," said Bob.

"They couldn't help it. We really should have come in yesterday, Bob. Come on, Fluffie, we'll find you something to eat. Oh, I say! Bob! Look what mum and dad have gone and done! They've left the kitchen door shut. No wonder Fluffie was taken short!"

"It stinks, this place," said Bob. He had sat down, I was very happy to notice, on the settee, and was wondering where the stench came from.

Tracy called my brother and me to the kitchen. We were

so hungry that we had almost reached starvation level: or so it felt. If you go for a certain length of time without eating, the hunger grows more and more intense, but you reach a point where you no longer want to eat. The smell of the tin she was opening was nauseating to me. Nevertheless we ate up what she put on our plates in greedy haste.

"Such nice weather too," she shouted back into the sitting-room, evidently continuing some conversation she had been having earlier with Bob.

"You mean, we could be down in Bournemouth now, if it wasn't for these cats," said Bob.

"I know," she said.

"Couldn't you get the neighbours to feed them?"

"You know what mum's like about Mrs Watkin – wouldn't have her in the house."

"Oh ——" Bob shouted out a very rude, but as it happened a very apposite word. He had just moved slightly on the settee and discovered what he was sitting in. "I'll kill those —— cats," he said. "I'll kill them."

"Bob! They couldn't help it," said Tracy. "Mum had locked them out of the kitchen." Just at that point, I felt the meat reacting badly with my empty stomach, and I started to heave and cough and retch.

"That's all we need," said Bob. "Darling Fluffie being sick."

They sponged and rubbed and mopped, but even so, what with the hall carpet, and the settee, and (now) Bob's trousers, there were quite a lot of dirty areas in the house, and the pong was pretty appalling. I did not really blame them for being angry. But nor did I begin to guess how angry Bob was.

When they had gone, leaving the kitchen door open this time, and a bowl of biscuits and a dish of milk, my brother came out of hiding from June's bedroom, and said, "What was all that about their going to Bournemouth?"

"It sounds as though they would like to go away too, but they can't," I said. "Because of us."

"What was Bob shouting about? He sounded as though he'd sat in something."

When I told my brother, he was very amused and laughed loud and long. He shared my low opinion of Bob. We had quite a nice little evening together, pottering round the house. If only we had been allowed out! I could see so many tempting birds hopping about on the lawn outside, but we could do nothing except press our noses against the glass of the window pane and stare at them.

Then, later that evening, we heard the front door open once more.

"Very attentive," said my brother sarcastically. "They obviously don't want to risk having to mop up after us again."

"That's not Tracy," I said.

"Who is it then?"

"It's Bob ... and another man."

Bob and the other man were talking much more loudly than usual. They were laughing and hiccoughing, and not walking very straight. There was a tendency to bump into things.

"Let's get it over with," said Bob. "Tracy would hate me if she knew I was doing this."

"It's easy," said the other young man, with a cruel laugh. "I've done it with several cats. You even get a taste for it after a while. Hello, my beauty!"

He crouched down and was addressing me. I felt all my fur stand up on end. This was an enemy. I did not know what he wanted to do to us, but I knew it wasn't nice.

"Have you got a bag we can put them in?" he asked Bob. "Preferably something that shuts. They put up a hell of a struggle sometimes."

"I still don't know what I'll say to Tracy," said Bob.

"Look, mate, do you want to come to Bournemouth, or don't you? A whole week in my caravan, you and the chick."

"Yeah, of course I want to come to Bournemouth."

"Well then. And you don't want to come back to the house and find all the mess left by these little darlings, do you? Hello, diddums!"

My brother, too, had arched his back, and fluffed out his tail.

"It's just that I don't know what I'll say to Tracy."

"I've told you. You let the cats out of the back door. You called and called, and they never come back."

I will give Bob the credit for being drunk, and not liking what he was doing. But the other young man was enjoying every second of it. He had gone into the kitchen, and found a couple of old shopping bags. Once we knew what he was up to, we gave him a run for his money.

My brother ran up to one of the bedrooms and hid in a favourite place of his on top of the wardrobe, while the two men, very drunk and very angry, chased me. They thought they had got me in the room June called the lounge, but Bob's friend stumbled against the potted plant on a stand and it, and he, fell to the ground. When he got up, he shouted, "I'll kill you!"

He had gloves on, and by the time he came clumping up the stairs after me, he had a bag in his hand, which fastened at the top with a zip. I was determined not to let him put me into it, but I stupidly ran into the bathroom, where there was nowhere to hide. I cowered under the wash basin, and heard his footsteps approaching.

"It went in here," he said.

"Is that Fluffie?" asked Bob.

"The moggy one. It's wild this one, should have been killed long ago."

"I'll look for Bootsie," said Bob gloomily.

The bathroom door opened, and Bob's horrible friend came in. I looked at him: hobnail boots, jeans, a blue jacket, leather motorcycling gloves on his hands. There was no part of him except the face which I could attack. As he crouched down with the open bag, however, his face was quite close to mine, and I sprang at him with open claws. I managed to take a bit out of his cheek, but it only made him angrier. He biffed me with his fist, and I was stunned by the blow. He did not knock me out, but the pain immobilized me and in that second he scooped me up and put me in the bag. I struggled and wriggled, but he was too strong for me, pressing my paws and my head down into the confines of the hateful bag.

"We'll have to leave Bootsie," Bob was calling from the bedroom. "He's on top of the wardrobe and he won't come down."

"Don't be so stupid," said Horrible. "I'll deal with it."

I heard them banging, and moving chairs around and cursing. Evidently, my brother escaped them at first, but they had shut the bedroom door and, however much of a fight he put up, it was hopeless against the two of them. All I was aware of in the darkness of the bag, was of being humped downstairs as if I were rubbish.

By now Bob was saying, "I don't like this," and Horrible was laughing. It was so dark and airless in my bag that I did not know exactly when we got outside. But eventually I was aware of being hurled into what must have been the back of an engine of murder, a car. I could dimly feel, through my bag, the sides of another bag, and I could hear my brother's muffled cries of protest.

"You drive, and I'll deal with them," said Horrible. "I don't want you making a mess of this."

"Where to?"

"Ring road, of course, how often do I have to tell you?"

The car roared off. I did not listen particularly to the chat which passed between the two friends. For much of the time they were silent. We could hear only the car engine, and the music on the box of voices. We stopped, and started, and stopped and moved off again. I felt sick, as I always do in cars. But this time it was not just the movement of the car. I felt sick with fury that these oafs could treat us in this way; sick with the knowledge that we could do nothing to stop them and that, whatever was going to happen, we could never have our revenge upon them; sick with the whole meaningless pain of existence.

The journey wasn't a long one. Eventually, I could hear Horrible wriggling about beside me, and saying "Right, my beauty." The car had slowed down a bit, and I think I heard my brother yelping with despair. Then, all of a sudden, the top of the bag was unzipped, and Horrible said, "Now your turn. It's a proper little savage, this one is."

He got me by the scruff of the neck. I saw that the car window was wide open, and because we were still moving along at some speed, a strong wind was blowing in my face.

"Out you go!" he shouted, and with a violent gesture, flung me out.

By an extraordinary stroke of luck, I landed on a grass verge, but with a great bump against my side. The shock of the thing made it hard to take in what had happened, and for a while, I lay there, with an acute pain in one of my back legs, crying with anger on the grass, as the cars and lorries roared past. After what could have been a few minutes or could have been some hours – it was quite impossible to guess the time – I thought of my brother. Where was he? Was he all right? I think in that first stupid moment, I assumed that because I was all right (or more or less all right) then he was probably alive and, if a bit battered, fit for the next stage of the adventure. I stood up. The pain in my back leg was excruciating, but I managed somehow to drag myself along. I do not know where I thought I was going, but it was good to be able to move, however painful it was. And then, in the darkness, I saw it. At first I thought it might have been some other animal, but the shape of his head could be made out on the road, perfectly still. I am sure that the Great Stillness – the mystery which he and I had watched coming upon Granny Harris – had already come upon him then, but at that moment, a bus thundered over his body and there could be no doubt that he was done for.

I would like to be able to tell you that I decided then and there, that I would never again trust human beings; that I decided as I watched my poor brother being mangled, like a piece of roadside litter, that I would lead an independent life, and trust only to myself, and to the mysteries which govern our lives. But I was in no mood for grand resolutions. There have been three great griefs in my life. The first was so confusing that I did not take it in at the time, but now I think of it as a great grief: it is when I was separated from my mother. The second grief was also confusing, but I felt all its fullness at the time, it was the fate of my brother on that road. In a blinding moment of horror I knew that I had lost my best friend in all the world, a friend who could never be replaced. And the third grief lay in the future. I did not stay to look back. I hobbled up a verge, through a fence, and over the corner of a field. I had no idea where I was going or what I was doing. For a moment of despair, I thought I had merely walked round in a circle, for having cut across the corner of the field, I found myself on the verge of another road. This time it seemed quieter. My leg wouldn't be dragged any further. I lay down, the most dejected, the most impotently angry, the most miserable cat in the world. And because I had no strength left, I lay there, even when a car slowed down and stopped; even when a torch shone in my eyes, and a female human voice said, "It's still alive, you know," my claws went out, but the struggle which I put up was merely notional. I was barely conscious when I was lifted up, and put into the back of another car.

CHAPTER TEN

When I came to, the pain was much less bad, but my leg still hurt. I leaned over to lick it, still with my eyes half shut, and was surprised to find that it had turned to cloth and wood. Then I realized it had been bandaged up. Opening my eyes, I found that I was lying in a blanket, on a floor of red, highly polished tiles. The room was warm and clean. From a window, the clear rays of the sun were pouring in. Just near the basket, there was a saucerful of milk. I got up – it felt strange, standing up on a splint – and hobbled over to have a drink. It felt good. It felt almost as good as that first day when I opened my eyes and realized for the week or so past, I had had this wonderful experience: I had been born! I was alive. Of course, it could not be quite as strange as that, but it was certainly more abundantly joyful. After all, I had come so close to *not* being alive, so close to the stillness which now embraced my brother.

The memory of him, which came back to me as I lapped up the milk, was particularly painful, and spoilt half the pleasure of coming back to life again. And then the whole sad story came back to me – of Tracy and the moronic Bob and his horrible friend; the bags, the car, the open window, the calamity. And now here I was. But where that was, I had no idea, and I had no reason to think that the new human beings – if they were human beings, who had tied this bandaging round me, and given me a blanket and milk – were to be trusted. After all, I was a prisoner here. Was there a way out?

The tiles were so highly polished, that I almost skidded on them. But, yes, I could walk again! It felt like quite an achievement. It was while I was taking my first tentative

85

steps, that the door opened and a female human being entered, wearing a long sort of black dress, and with a long veil draped over her head. She had a cross round her neck and a little triangle of red at the breast. Never having seen a human being dressed in this way, I was a little bit surprised. Normally you see their legs, but with this one you just saw highly polished black shoes; no legs at all.

In a calm, friendly voice, which made me almost regret having raised all my hackles and stuck my tail fiercely in the air, the strange person said, "So you're awake!"

And then she vanished again, and I could hear her voice in a corridor saying excitedly, "She's awake! She's recovered. Sister, come and see, Mildred's awake!"

Mildred?

She?

Though still in a very weak condition, my interest quickened. Evidently, I was sharing a room with another cat, a female cat, and my interest in female cats is always strong. What was this Mildred like? I began to picture her in my imagination. Perhaps she was a silly piece of white fluff, with teasing blue eyes, and a seductively simpering little voice. (Howling on a shed roof one night, months ago, I had felt wild about such a cat! Not Princess, but another.) Or perhaps she was beautifully sleek and black and plump, with green eyes? Or perhaps she was a Siamese? But somehow, I could not imagine even a human being deciding to call a Siamese cat Mildred. I looked around the room and apart from the basket, a table and two upright chairs it was, so far as I could see, quite empty. So where was Mildred? On the table top? With great effort, I saw if I could spring up on to the chair, but there was no bounce in my back legs, and even if there had been, jumping would not have been easy with my bandage and splint. I ended merely by landing on the floor, with an excruciating twinge of pain. However I pulled myself up again and tottered towards the fireplace, from whence I could get a good view of the table top. No Mildred there.

It was strange. The female personage in the long flowing clothes had most definitely said, "Sister, come and see, Mildred's awake."

In a few minutes, the lady returned with her sister, who was dressed, rather surprisingly, in exactly the same manner as the other lady: no legs, just shiny shoes, and a long grey dress: at the neck, the same triangle of red, and the same dangling cross, and a long piece of cloth instead of fur on their heads.

"You see, Sister, she really is awake."

"Hello, Mildred," said the lady's sister.

After my visit to the by-pass with Bob and Horrible, I shall always be nervous of human beings. But, as you may understand, at that point, I was more than nervous. Even specimens as apparently kind and bland as these two were to be treated with the utmost caution. When one crouched down – and I could not really tell whether it was the first lady, or her sister – and stretched out a clean and well washed hand, I hissed and made to scratch it.

"You see, she's terrified."

"But cats are all the same."

"How can people *do* it?"

"Well, Mildred, at least you're alive."

I hissed again, to warn them to keep their distance, but it nevertheless fascinated me that, while looking quite firmly in my direction, the lady seemed to be having a discussion with this other, female cat, called Mildred.

At that point, I really did begin to think I was seeing things, because a *third* lady came into the room, and she was dressed in exactly the same way as the others! The only difference was that she had glass in frames, balanced on her nose and covering her eyes, the way that some people do.

"Sister Caroline Mary, just *look* at this beautiful creature," said one of the ladies. So this was another sister! How many sisters were there in this family?

"I've called her Mildred," said the first lady. "The vet said that if she came round from this sleep, she'd have a good chance of recovery."

"Did the vet really say that, Sister?" asked Sister Caroline Mary.

"Why do you ask, Sister?"

"I mean, did he really say that if *she* came round from her sleep, *she* would recover?"

"I don't know what you mean. I don't remember the vet's exact words..."

"Because I think, Sister, that Mildred is really a Miles."

And the three women laughed very much.

Really a Miles? This was even more peculiar? It took me some time to realize that they were not just looking at me, they were talking about me. I was "Mildred", now I was "Miles". What *is* this human craze for naming things? Where does it come from? I find it all very hard to understand, though I know that you, little Grandkitten, have adopted it, and are happy to be known by the name your human friends call you by.

"I think he's a tom," said the Sister with eye-glasses. "He's big enough. He looks a strong chap. I wonder if he'll stay."

In the days that followed, I saw more of this Sister with glasses. She would come into my room and talk to me. At first I put up a show of hissing and spitting at her, and threatening to claw her if she came near me. She said she quite knew how I felt, and that often, she wanted to claw and spit and hiss at human beings, even though she had never been thrown out of a car by one. She said that anyone who sat near Sister Antonia Mary in choir and heard her sing sharp five times a day for a week would want to claw her; and that the least you could do was hiss at Sister Pamela Mary when she burnt the fish cakes and served them up with mashed potatoes and mashed swede, and no vitamins at all – and the cabbage cooked for hours, no fresh salad. The Sister with glasses, whom the others called Sister Caroline Mary, told me that she would love an orange and she wondered what I would most love. A kidney? It is not literally true that this Sister and I spoke the same language. But when she started to talk about kidneys, I stood up and very very cautiously rubbed myself against the part of her dress where legs would be on another human being. And she said, "We'll see what we can do." I did not let her tickle my head on that occasion. Indeed, when she tried to do so, I hissed once more, but it was not very consistent, since I had rubbed myself against her dress, and even purred a little bit.

Each day, I was getting stronger, and the next day, I wandered out into the neat little garden which the Sisters called the garth. It was really astonishing to see the size of this family. There were about twenty Sisters, and they were all dressed in exactly the same way. Moreover, their mother, or the one they called their mother, looked astonishingly young, not much older than three or four, I would think, in cat years. It was she, the young mother, who looked younger in fact than her daughter Caroline Mary, who said sedately but firmly one day, "Sister, do you have to run about the cloister as if you had a train to catch?"

"I'm sorry, Mother."

"How's that cat you're so fond of?"

"It was him I was looking for, Mother. The butcher's boy has just been, and brought a surprise for him."

I limped across the garth towards my friend.

"You know, Sister, it is almost as if that animal understands us."

"*Almost*, Mother?"

Sister Caroline Mary led the way to the kitchen. The legendary Sister Pamela Mary, about whom I had heard so much, was there, unwrapping some chickens and lots of sausages which she had collected from the butcher's boy at a side gate. The air was heavy with cabbage steam.

"Sister," she said snappishly, "having that cat in my kitchen is one thing I will not allow."

"If I could simply borrow a knife, Sister? To cut up a couple of kidneys."

A couple? Oh, this was good news.

"Have you Mother's permission for this?" asked the scandalized Sister Pamela Mary.

"I have Mother's full permission and authority. Miles is now part of the community."

"It's absurd to talk like that," said Sister Pamela Mary. "Besides how can a male cat be part of us? No man is allowed in the enclosure. Why should a male cat?"

"Most of the Sisters still think Miles is a she-cat called Mildred," laughed my friend. "And anyway, we allow our Father Warden and other priests into the enclosure."

"Miles isn't a priest," said Sister Pamela Mary.

"But his ancestors were worshipped as Gods, somewhere in Egypt," said Sister Caroline Mary. "I think that beats being a priest of the Church of England."

"Sister, you should be ashamed of yourself," said Sister Pamela Mary.

But she did allow Sister Caroline Mary to cut up the kidneys with a knife and bring them in a saucer out into the garth. As we left the kitchen, Sister Pamela Mary called out harshly, "You're getting too fond of that animal, Sister, and it isn't sensible. They *never* stay."

Oh, those kidneys were good, and the warmth of the sun on my back in that quiet little enclosed garden. They were perfectly fresh kidneys, two large ones, rich and moist with blood. When I had eaten them and licked my lips, I felt very good indeed. Sister Caroline Mary was sitting on a sort of stone window ledge in the cloister. Her face wore a look of detached contentment which made me have a curious thought which I have never had before or since about a human being. I thought, "Now here sits a very happy cat," and it was only after a few moments that I realized the absurdity of my thought. Sister Caroline Mary was very much like a cat. I suppose that was why I found her so companionable. I had still not quite let her pet me or cuddle me. I had only rubbed myself against her dress (she called it a habit) and purred when she scratched my head. But now, with the warmth of the sun on my fur, and a feeling of contentment and well-being spreading through my body, it seemed perfectly natural to go and sit on Sister's lap, and allow her to stroke my head and back. And I had vowed that I would never trust another human being again; and all it had taken, on this occasion, to crack my resolve, was a splint and a bandage, and a week of kind words, warmth and decent treatment. Perhaps I was not yet ready to be a hero. And, of course, at that stage, my adventures had only just begun.

I was interested by what Sister Pamela Mary had had to say – "They never stay." Who were these mysterious *they*? And why did they not stay? Sister Caroline Mary was a talkative person, even though I gathered from what she told me that the Sisters were not supposed to talk much to one another. Why not? It seemed a strange idea. Anyway, they weren't. And once I was settled on her lap, she told me all over again what a bad cook Sister Pamela Mary was, and how she was really a very annoying person, and what a lucky thing it was that she, Sister Caroline Mary, had not lost her temper with Sister Pamela Mary.

"And anyway, it isn't true that they don't all stay. Hattie stayed with us until she died – she was with us seven years, and such a friend of mine. It's because we are so near the bypass you see. These *wicked* people throw cats out of car windows. I'm afraid that you are by no means the first to come to us. We do not keep all of you, otherwise we should have as many cats as we do Sisters (which I should like, but it would not suit all our Sisters). Some of you, we manage to find homes for; and others – yes, others do decide that it is time to move on. And I quite understand that. You're not like us. You haven't promised to stay here forever. Why should you? I just hope...' – her voice sounded as though it were about to crack with sadness – "that you don't decide to move on too soon, old chap. Now there's the bell for vespers."

And she lifted me gently to the ground before standing up

and walking round the cloister to the darkened room at the end, where, every time the bell rang, at all hours of the day and night, the Sisters assembled. I decided to follow her on this occasion, hoping that no one had any objection, but not really caring in particular whether they had an objection or not. They all assembled outside in one room, and then filed into this other, darker room, first of all bowing towards the end of the room which had a window in it, and then turning to face each other in straight rows. And then they began to sing in high-pitched peculiar voices. And yet something in their singing made me think of the two Sisters' quarrel in the kitchen, about how my ancestors had been Gods long ago in Egypt. And in the darkness, and the singing, and the thought of the Gods, and long ago, there was a sort of strangeness which both made the fur stand up on my back, and at the same time made me feel that this room was a comfortable sort of place to be. So I wandered up to the front, still limping quite badly, and thought that I would sit on the step and watch them all bowing and singing.

But as I did so, the singing changed to another noise. Oh, they were still trying to sing. But the noise which was coming out of their mouths was very different. They were all convulsed with the sound they call laughter. Now what was making them laugh, I could not make out. I looked around, and as far as I could see there was nothing funny happening. As best as they gigglingly could, they finished chanting from their books, and then they filed out again. But one of the Sisters came up to me afterwards, and said, "Mildred, dear, you had us all in stitches. Can you warn us next time you want to come to chapel?"

Very strange creatures, human beings are.

For a cat of a different breed or temperament, I dare say that life with the Sisters would have been a distinct possibility – life for ever I mean. There seemed to be no marauders there, no engines of murder, nor Horribles. Presumably, like the Sisters, I could have stayed there for ever, and escaped

92

the Great Stillness, the Stillness which had taken Granny Harris and my brother.

And yet, as I got better, I knew that Sister Caroline Mary was right, and that it would not suit me to stay there for ever. I began to miss other cats. And I also began to miss – well, the sense you live with all the time if you are on your own and on the road: freedom, danger, independence, all those things, a sense that each day is going to be different, each day a little bit frightening. Among the Sisters, as far as I could tell, each day was the same. I think it was supposed to be. But it was not my nature to sit peacefully in the sun, to think that I had an adventure if I chased one sparrow, to regard the arrival of the butcher's boy as the high point of my week, to see no other cats. I started to mind about that very much after a couple of weeks. I began to sense in the air that there were hundreds of other cats in the world, and that, though I would always be alone, I belonged not with human beings, but with my own kind. The summer breezes at evening brought wild thoughts and sometimes, a wonderful scent, which I cannot describe to you, but which made me think of beautiful female cats.

And yet, those Sisters had become my friends, and their place had become something very like a home. My leg was very nearly completely mended now. The splint and bandages had been removed, and I had started to be more adventurous in my exploring. I saw that by climbing over one of the garden walls, I could easily get into a paddock, and beyond that there were other human habitations. On the other side of the Sisters' house, moreover, by climbing a wooden fence, I could get into a gravel drive, at the end of which was a road, a long straight road, leading to a town with a castle at the top of it. I could not help thinking of Sister Pamela's words when we went into the kitchen, Sister Caroline Mary and I: "You're getting too fond of that animal, Sister." It is true. And I was getting too fond of her. Far too fond. It does not do, if you want to lead a wandering life like mine, to go getting fond of other beings, still less of people. And as I keep telling you, I have had little enough cause to be fond, in general, of people. But I was fond of Sister Caroline Mary. So fond, that I did not want to cause her any more pain. It was obviously best, if I was to go, that I should go soon. Nor could I quite bear to warn her. Surely she would try to dissuade me, to hold me back; and that would do no good. It would only delay the moment of agony, the moment when I had to be on the road again.

I decided to go at night, and not to make any plans, but just to leave, when the impulse took me. Sister Caroline Mary had already told me, in the course of our strange little chats, that the Sisters were not allowed outside the enclosure of the house and garden, so once I was over the wall, I was safe. There would be no heartbreaking farewells. In the early days and weeks of my recovery I had felt so grateful to her. But now I did not feel I was leaving a "benefactor" or a creature of a different species who had condescended to be kind to me. I felt merely that I was leaving a friend; perhaps the last friend I was ever to have in this world; and why I was doing so was a mystery to me. I only knew that I had to. Nothing would hold me back.

It was a beautiful warm summer night. The air was like nectar. The night-scented stock and the tobacco plants in the garth filled the air with sweetness. The sky was a rich dark blue, as it is in the summer night, and our great Mother-of-Night was in her fullness, casting a white light and deep shadows about the garth. Her sisters the stars shone, not with that cold sparkling brightness which they have in winter on clear frosty nights, but with warmth, almost like candles lit at distant windows. And in that scented night air, there came into my nostrils the unmistakable knowledge that somewhere, somewhere quite close if I could only find her, there she was. She, the cat of my dreams, whom I must woo, and find, and love. I stood and listened. In the far distance, I could almost discern – or was it my imagination – her voice calling to me through the warm air, wailing her beautiful song of love.

I waited. A bell rang once more, and the Sisters all trooped into the chapel, and for a while, the sound of my mysterious beloved – if such it was – was drowned by the noise of the Sisters, singing their songs. Perhaps they too, in their way, were songs of love, but not my sort of love. If only there had been some way of explaining, some way of saying to Sister Caroline Mary that I had no intention, in leaving her, of spurning her or rejecting her. I was not treating her as Bob and Horrible had treated me. And yet, and yet. Leaving the place made me feel as if that were just what I was doing. I stayed, thinking about it too long, perhaps, unable to stop myself listening for one last time, to the mysterious distant chanting of those human female voices, singing their songs by night. And then I left. I arose and walked along the top of the wooden fence which led to the drive, and crunched down the gravel. The road was not the best place for me to walk, but it had grass verges and ditches where I could hide if a car came, and in the distant town where the castle was, I knew there would be cats. It was, perhaps, from there that she was to be found. I looked furtively to left and to right, and then, up the straight moonlit road towards the town and castle. "Goodbye, dear friend," I said, and then at a brisk pace I set off down the road. When I had run a long way – perhaps a hundred yards, I looked back. And then I knew that Sister Caroline Mary had, after all, understood. For she was breaking her rules, just for me. And there she stood, with the moonlight falling on her veil and habit, looking even more cat-like in the rays of our Mother-of-Night. Her hand was raised, but she was not summoning me back. She was waving a farewell and – who knows, perhaps too, a blessing.

CHAPTER ELEVEN

I found Her – the cat whom I had heard and smelt on the night air, not a quarter of a mile down the road. As on almost all these occasions, it was more fun imagining what she was like *before* I met her than when we actually met. Still, any port in a storm. It served. And I daresay that I would have happier memories of the little thing – she was grey, I seem to remember and she smelt of the paper chimneys her minder smoked – had not the minder, a furious apparition with dyed yellow fluff on her head shaped a bit like a helmet opened her window and thrown a bucket of water over me during my very passable attempts to sing Little Grey a love song of my own composing.

"And don't come back! Go and molest someone else's cat!" she shrieked. "Tootles! Come in at once! I told you..." – she shouted back crossly to some person who was obviously in the room with her – "not to let Tootles out tonight."

"Madam!" I called. "I would not dream of coming back. And as for molesting your cat, as you call her, I was merely..."

But the witticism was hardly worth another bucket of water, which would have hit me if I had not scuttled off the kitchen roof, down a drain pipe, and out again into the lane. Little Grey's mews and miaows as I left would have been flattering if they had been just for me. But she herself had got quite wet. And I understand any cat crying if it had to be locked up with such a creature as had appeared at the window.

I was now back in the savage world of human beings, with legs, paper chimneys, buckets of water, and a desire to make cat life as awkward and nasty as they could. It was a salutary moment. Such human beings are the norm, and one cannot remind oneself of it too often. The numbers who even like us are few; and as for those, like Sister Caroline Mary, who can almost talk our language – they are sadly even fewer. Once out in the lane, I toddled along quite happily through a sort of suburb. There was only one nasty moment, and that was when, feeling rather hungry, I thought that I would go round the back of a house and see what had been put in the dustbin. As I approached, there was the most appetizing reek of a decomposing fowl – though three-quarters ruined by cooking, of course. Sister Caroline Mary always said that Sister Pamela Mary spoilt food by cooking it, and I think as a general principle all food is wrecked by cooking, especially meat. Why do they do it? Put a chicken in an oven for an hour and the greater part of its goodness is gone; there's no blood left in it, and all its flesh turns a revolting white. I notice, Grandkitten, that you have a decadent taste for cooked meat. You should guard against it.

Anyway, the bin which I approached, definitely did contain a chicken carcass, and from the delicious smell I thought it quite possible it might be encrusted with a decent relish of lice or worms. I jumped and got the lid off the thing with no difficulty, and in that split second, I am thankful to say, I looked back over my shoulder before sinking my teeth into the joint. It was, indeed, quite rotten, and what is more there was a lot of meat left on it. But there, in the yard behind me, I saw hostile eyes. A dog? But a dog would have barked. And then it sprang out into the moonlight, and made for me. I saw that it was a large dog fox, with sharp yellowing teeth. It gave off the most appalling stench, incidentally, almost human in its disgustingness. It had some of that human mustiness – you know what I mean. And there was no doubt at all that it meant, not merely to scare me off, but to get me.

Foxes are dangerous beasts. Like cats, they enjoy hunting

for its own sake, but they don't play fair. We very rarely kill something which we would not want to eat, or which it is not perfectly good sportsmanship to kill. I know that there are cats who are so pathetically "humanized" that they teach their children that it is wrong to kill hamsters and guinea-pigs. Personally, I have no sympathy with this anti-hunting lobby. What are our victims for if they aren't to be chased? A good day's sport is the finest exercise which a cat can have. But your fox is quite a different creature. He plays dirty. He treats us as he might treat a vole or a mouse. He is prepared to terrorize and maim us before he kills us. With us, this is all part of the time-honoured ritual of hunting, and for my part I think it would be a crying shame if it were ever altered. But there is something very disgusting about creatures who would play the same pranks on us. What is more, I do not think that foxes ever eat cats. They merely bite us in the throat, after playing with us, because they are jealous of our vitality and wish to reduce us to the great stillness.

This fiendish fox really flew at me. My tail even brushed its filthy face as I jumped in the air. Mercifully, there was a windowbox above the dustbin, and above the windowbox a drain pipe. Having climbed up the drain pipe a little way I could jump onto a wall, and look down at the fox in the yard, staring up at me and baring its revolting teeth. How would they like to be chased and hunted as if they were vermin? I bet they have never thought of that!

You sometimes hear older human beings telling their children about cunning foxes or clever foxes. This one wasn't cunning. It stood there, like the stupidest dog, waiting for me to come off the wall. Oh yes, Reynard! Very likely, isn't it, that I am going to jump down into your jaws.

Just to show what I thought of the brute, I hissed and spat a bit. After a while, however, it seemed sensible simply to sit quietly until he got bored and sloped off. As indeed he did. But now, would you credit what happened next? A man opened the back door of the house and peered into the darkness. Then a voice – a woman's voice – came from the lighted hallway. "Can you see it?"

"No, but I'm sure it's here somewhere. I'll go and look at the dustbins."

I have heard it said that people train dogs to hunt foxes. They put peaked black helmets on their fur, and red coats on their backs, and they ride round fields on horseback blowing trumpets, while their dogs chase the fox to his lair. It is amusing to us to think that they can think of this as hunting. For me, the very essence of hunting is to do it yourself, and not to train a pack of silly hounds to do it for you. If a man had the excitement, first of smelling the fox, and then of creeping up on it unawares, then of pouncing upon it and playing with it; finally, killing it and eating the meat fresh and warm, then I could understand his desire to hunt. But I do wonder whether it is true that man is a hunting animal. My evidence is all to the contrary. Man is too clumsy and too unobservant to be a hunter. While I can believe that some men enjoy killing foxes for pleasure (and killing for pleasure is hardly the same as hunting) I have the evidence of my own eyes to show that some men believe these horrible animals to be their friends.

The man went down to the dustbins where I had been eating the chicken joint and called back, "Certainly some animal has been trying to get at it."

"It might have been a cat," called the woman.

"Mmmm." The man made a noise which was meant to show how clever he was. "Could be," he said sagely. "But I am sure I saw a fox."

"I've got some of that meat. He'll come back if we leave it by the back door," said the woman.

"Poor creature. If that *was* him trying to get into our dustbin, he must have been starving."

"I hope he didn't get that chicken. It was almost rotten."

I could hardly believe my ears during this conversation.

The man went into the house once more, and after a short while, he re-emerged with a tin plate and something on the plate which looked very appetizing indeed.

"He won't come if he thinks we're looking at him," said the woman.

"I know," said the man. "We'll put the plate so that we can see it from indoors, then we'll switch off all the lights in the house and watch."

They put the plate down by the back door, and then did as they said they would. This was too good an opportunity to miss! I came down off the top of the wall with the speed of light, grabbled what was on the plate into my jaws, and climbed up on to the top of the wall again.

The lights went on in the house once more.

By the back door, the man and woman appeared.

"Did you see that?"

"Can you match the cheek of it?"

"It shouldn't be too difficult to find."

"A cat? You must be joking. There are hundreds of strays living in this neighbourhood. They even form themselves into colonies, you know, and go out scavenging. But I've never seen anything quite so blatant as that."

"Well, I think we've lost our fox for tonight, darling."

"It's so annoying to think of it going to Mrs Vaughan-Townsend's garden."

"I know, darling. But he's our fox really."

"Of course he is."

I promise you that this is what they said. They really did think that because this greedy fox had strayed into a dustbin near their back door and was willing to eat their food that he was theirs. Can *you* understand this property-mania? I can't. I did not think that I owned them, merely because I had between my jaws an absolutely delicious piece of meat. Nor, come to that, did I particularly think that I owned the meat. But of one thing I was certain. I was going to eat that meat all by myself.

The top of the wall is no place for a feast. So, keeping to

the shadows as much as possible, and treading with the lightest of steps, I made my way out through a hedge at the back of these people's garden. Then I got to a species of rough ground, and for the first time in my flight, I thought it was safe to let the meat drop from my jaws. You will think I am exaggerating when I tell you that it was very good lean meat, the size of a kitten like yourself. These *idiots* had put a pound and a half of good raw meat for Mr Reynard! Can you *credit* it?

There is one thing that I envy the human race, and that is that it wears clothes with pockets. Even for a cat with my voracious appetite, it would have been out of the question to eat all of this meat in one go. On the other hand, I knew that if I ate my fill and then hid it, coming back for more when I was hungry, the meat would be found by someone else. If only I could have had a pocket in which to keep the extra meat until I was hungry again.

Anyway, I put the steak on the ground, and took a small mouthful of fat from the edge. It was delicious. Very gingerly, I tugged at a bit of side gristle, and then I sank my teeth into a succulently red piece of the meat itself. It was the sort of meat which they often eat in their kitchens; from which beast it comes, I cannot guess, though I think it might be a big dog. It is anyhow delicious. But my enjoyment of this particular piece of meat was to be short lived, for in the middle of my mouthful I was suddenly conscious that I was being watched, and the voice of a rather uncultivated cat said, "Like to share that, friend?"

I digested my mouthful while, instinctively my hackles rose, and my tail became straight as a poker. I grabbed the meat into my mouth. I sensed from that voice and that question, that there was danger, very great danger in the air.

"Now, come on, friend, be reasonable," said the voice.

I, with the meat between my jaws, said nothing.

"You have been living too much among the Yoomans, you 'ave. Share and share alike's our motto. Each cat has no identity of himself. He merely exists to share and help other

101

cats. Now this grabbing all the meat for yourself. It's a Yooman thing to do. So drop it, brother."

I looked into the darkness, and I could see some red eyes glaring at me. They were expressionless, horrible eyes. I saw no reason for sharing the meat with him. This was not because I regarded the meat as mine and mine alone. It was a lucky find, and if I met a cat who made himself – or herself – agreeable to me, I should have shared the meat quite happily. It was this sinister tone of voice which made me angry, and the knowledge that he meant me no good.

Instinct was right. The voice had turned to a hiss.

"I must ask you again, brother, to drop that meat."

Now the horrifying thing about this, was the voice came from behind me. The red eyes into which I was staring were silent. So, there were two of them. At least two of them. The truth of this had only just dawned on me when I felt a tremendous blow on the back of my head. A filthy and strong cat with claws out had jumped on my back and was trying to pull me over backwards. In turning, I wrenched a shoulder – not badly, but the momentary twinge of pain was enough to give him an advantage over me. I struck out with my claws, but my blow was off target. I hit his side. He'd got the back of my head. By then, red-eyes was coming at me from the front. I did manage to get in a good blow against him, to judge by the screech of pain he let out. But by then, of course, I had dropped the meat and started to squeal myself.

I could not see in the dark exactly how big they were, but they were obviously full grown and every bit as big as me. The loss of the meat was sad. But by now I was not thinking of it so much, as of how to get away from these cats as quickly as possible. I decided that I would let them have the meat, and while they were fighting over it among themselves, I should be able to escape into the unknown darkness of the night.

I had completely misjudged the situation. The cat who had attacked me from behind, and who had, in the course of our fight, bitten off half my ear, had been joined by a second, and with the pair of them sitting on my back, I had nothing for it but to sit – or rather lie down quietly. I assumed that the cat on my back had been joined by red-eyes, but when I opened my own eyes, those horrible red eyes were still staring at me.

"Not a bad fighter," said red-eyes. "Not bad, that is, for someone who has been completely corrupted and adapted himself to Yooman values. You must learn to share everything with your brother cats, brother."

"My brother is dead," I said. "He was killed by human beings in the most brutal way. I am no friend of man. I live in no human household. I acknowledge no master beneath our great mother the moon..."

At the mention of the moon, one of the thugs on my back cuffed my bleeding half-ear.

"That's Yooman language, brother," said red-eyes. "Indypandants is what they calls it. They lies, and we do not talk of the moon, brother."

"Why not?" I asked. "It is she who lights our night. It is she who shines down upon us when we make love, and who guides our path..." But I wasn't allowed to finish the sentence. What was the point, anyway, with this oaf and his bully-boys?

"Cats isn't indy or pendant," said red-eyes.

"Independent? But all creatures *are* independent," I said. "Some, like the human race and the ants seem to need to huddle together in clusters or cloisters in order to survive. Others, like cats, are essentially loners..."

Once more I was cuffed on the head from behind.

"Cats isn't indy or pendant," said red-eyes again. Since he was, strictly speaking, talking nonsense, there was nothing to argue with. Even if I had felt inclined to dispute his point of view, the presence of the two bullies on my back acted as a powerful disincentive.

"Shall we finish him?" asked one of the cats on my back.

"Like I said," said red-eyes, "this is not a bad fighter. He

103

isn't an old cat. How old are you?"

"I'm not sure," I said truthfully.

"You're a young cat," said red-eyes. "You haven't learnt to count."

On closer acquaintance with red-eyes, I found that he had adopted – albeit crudely and stupidly – a whole range of human assumptions and values, including his desire to compute cycles of our mother the moon and call them Time. But he was so acclimatized to the human world (while thinking himself independent of it) that he did not know what had happened.

"You are young," red-eyes repeated, "and our brotherhood needs youth. You are young and you can unlearn the Yooman nonsense which you have been taught by your corrupt and bombinabel Yooman masters. You are welcome to join our brotherhood, brother."

This was terrible. Evidently these low-grade cats had ganged together into some kind of club and were expecting me to join them. The reason was not hard to seek. It lay before us in the moonlight, on the rubble and rough ground, in the shape of a juicy piece of steak.

"Anyone who can provide nourishment like this is a welcome member of the brotherhood," said red-eyes.

"I'm most awfully grateful for the offer," I said.

"Good," said red-eyes.

"But I think I would be happier . . . that is to say, I think it would be more suitable if I continued to strike out on my own. There's nothing I would like more than to belong to your brotherhood —"

"Good," said red-eyes. "Then that settles it. You come along with us."

"No," I said. "Hear me out."

"No is not a word which a younger brother says to an older brother," said one of the oafs on my back, digging his claws into my shoulder blade.

"I was going to say that while I was – ouch – flattered to

104

be asked to join you — I really want to stay on my own."

"Indy-pandant?" red-eyes said the words as a joke.

"We likes steaks," said the two oafs on my back in unison.

"You have already proved yourself useful, brother. Now you must come along and see where you lives."

"Move," said one of the oafs. The other had jumped off my back and picked up the bit of steak and put it into his own mouth.

"Now mind, Twinkle," said red-eyes to the oaf with the steak in his mouth. "We want all that meat brought home to the Commune. No nibbling along the way."

"Right, Tom-Cat."

It was with horror that I soon discovered that all the cats in the Commune called each other by names. Some actually chose to be called by the name they had been given by their human masters. Others who had lived in the wild all their lives pathetically tried to ape this habit, like red-eyes, who had never lived in human ownership, but who was most insistent that we should all call him Tom-Cat.

"But it is just what they call male cats," I said to one of the younger cats in the Commune.

"There is only one Tom-Cat," said this young sycophant, and the pathetic thing is, he really believed it.

Sometimes, they called him Our Father Tom-Cat, and sometimes, Our Tom.

The brotherhood encamped in the remains of an old concrete garage which stood on the edge of a desolate bit of ground where red-eyes (or Tom-Cat as I now learned to call him) and his two henchman brought me. I went with them that night because I was a fool. It might have involved a nasty fight, but I think that I could have got away from them that night in the dark. But the moral pressure of red-eyes, and the actual pressure of Carrot's claws made it difficult to refuse their offer of accommodation for the rest of the night. When we got there, it was, in fact, rather welcoming. The meat was torn up and shared round among what seemed, in the dark, like a lot of cats. After that, without any more worry, I fell asleep. It was light when I woke up.

And it was in the light, during the first few days of my membership of the brotherhood, that I began to size the whole thing up.

CHAPTER TWELVE

There was one thing which you would find it hard to understand about the Commune; and that is, why we all submitted to it – for day after day, month after month. Some of the cats had been there for years. They had lost all desire for freedom or independence or a proper feline existence and they accepted Tom-Cat's authority without question. The Commune was described as a brotherhood, and we were all obliged to call each other brother (even the female cats were called brother). But nothing was less like brotherhood. The whole structure of life in the Commune was hierarchical. Tom-Cat ruled it with an absolute authority which would have been the envy of any human sultan or tyrant. If any cat threatened to step out of line (and few did), Tom-Cat's bullying guards made them pretty soon regret it. Absolute rebellion was almost unheard of, though a poor thin cat, about my colouring, half my size, once tried to whisper to me the story of how six cats had, years before, attempted to overthrow Tom-Cat, and been themselves defeated. They had mysteriously disappeared one night and afterwards it became a crime to name them – even though they had once been Tom-Cat's favourites. Soon enough, their memory faded and there were no cats old enough to remember The Rebels. The smallest insubordination was punished. If you complained about the mingy food rations you might find yourself being starved for two or three days. If you chased after a beautiful female cat you had to make sure that she was not "answered for" by one of the thuggish brutes in Tom-Cat's good books. And, of course, straying "outside bounds" was strictly forbidden. Any poor cat who thought of *escaping* the Commune was dragged back by Tom-Cat's henchmen, and beaten and starved and made to repeat Tom-Cat's nonsensical formula which they called his "thoughts".

There is no moon. There are no stars. Tom-Cat is our only light. Indy is a Yooman Pandance. Yooman names degrades the brotherhood, but it is a privilege to bear names for the sake of our brother Tom-Cat.

This was the sort of drivel which young kittens were taught to lisp by their anxious mothers.

Things had so transpired that the majority of cats in the Commune, although they could not possibly have *enjoyed* life there, were terrified of anything which threatened it. They must have known with one part of themselves that Tom-Cat was a tyrant and a bully who was organizing a hateful system ruled over by a small gang of thugs. But with another part of themselves, they believed that it was their duty to spy on one another, to tell Tom-Cat's thugs stories about their friends, even against their own children. For without Tom-Cat, they believed, there would be chaos, without Tom-Cat they would be taken into slavery; *without Tom-Cat we should starve* were words which every member of the Commune was obliged to say before eating his or her meagre meal. Above all, they believed that Tom-Cat had the power to save them from the Van, and it was the Van, even more than the merciless tyranny of Tom-Cat himself, which they feared. Presumably it was this *fear* which provides an answer to my question: *why did we submit to it?* We were afraid of what would happen if we did not.

The Commune was organized on these lines. Ten cats, either males or brother she-cats, would be sent out at regular intervals "on the prowl". It was their task to provide food for the fifteen or twenty other cats who stayed in the garage or its immediate environs. There was a rota system, so you might expect to be sent out on the "prowl" about twice a week. A fairly good way of getting an enemy into trouble was to drop a hint in the ear of one of Tom-Cat's favourites that this particular cat *ate* food while out on the prowl. It was a cardinal sin, punishable by three days' starvation, or even by death if Tom-Cat was in the mood for killing. *All* food found out on the prowl had to be brought back and given to Tom-Cat for the good of the Commune. No nibbling titbits on the way home. When the heap of rotten bones, old fish, decayed lamb chops or chickens had been laid at his feet, Tom-Cat would then decree how it was to be divided up. Preference was always given to the she-cats of whom he happened at that moment to be fond, or to the more sycophantic of his thuggish bodyguard. But the truth is, there was never quite enough food to go round. Even if Tom-Cat had not imposed his rigorous system of punishments by starvation, some cats would have in any case gone hungry. The advantage of the punishment system was that we all accepted it. Had there been no organization, only the weak would have starved, and fights would have broken out. By making us all fear and suspect each other, and by uniting us in a common fear of the Van, Tom-Cat did stop us fighting among ourselves. No small achievement. But I do not think he would have been able to do it without our common fear of the Van.

As I tell you about my time at the Commune – and I suppose that I must have been there quite some time – I feel that it is hard to imagine submitting to it all. What? I? With all my feelings of fierce independence? Would I not have preferred to fight to the death, to suffer the great stillness itself, rather than submit to the tyranny of a worthless bully like Tom-Cat? It now seems to me shameful that I did not resist, but I am sure that the reason Tom-Cat and his hench cats were able so easily to subdue me was that they had convinced me of the terrible danger of the Van. It was the thick-headed ginger (he liked us to call him Twinkle) who first told me of the Van.

"Yooman vans drive round and round – they are coming to get us," he said. "Our great brother Tom-Cat, and the only Tom-Cat, could drive a van if he wanted, but vans is yooman."

"Vans?" I asked. "What are you talking about?"

"Surely you have seen them roaring up the roads," piped in one of the more submissive little cats who was listening to my conversation with Twinkle.

"The engines of murder?" I asked. "I have been inside one. My brother was crushed by one. They are indeed very dangerous."

But Twinkle biffed me for saying this. "Vans is yooman, but the only Tom-Cat, our brother, has been inside one. You have never been inside a van."

"But I *have*. I didn't know they were called vans. My brother and I called them engines of murder."

"Only Tom-Cat can save us from the Van," said Twinkle.

"Or our own skill?" I asked.

"What's that? *Own? Skill?* What means?" asked the submissive little cat. He was a pathetic, skinny, scabby little chap – one of Tom-Cat's children, who had never known life outside the Commune. His complete ignorance of what it meant to do something on one's own struck a chill into my heart. And it was then that Twinkle spoke.

"Look," he said, with real urgency and forgetting the claptrap which loyalty to Tom-Cat made him spout. "You think only of the dangers of being *hit* by cars and vans as they roar up and down the roads. But there is a far worse danger than that. We do not fear *that* any more than the majority of cats fear it. But our brother Tom-Cat has discovered that there is one van to fear above all others. It drives round, not in order to hit us, but so as to *pick us up*. This Van has yoomans in it who want to capture us. We do not know exactly what they do to us when they catch us. Some say that they eat us alive..."

"But they don't," I said – thinking of Granny Harris's mild little television suppers or Sister Caroline Mary's overcooked refectory meals. "Human beings would never eat us alive..."

"Others think they take us to torture chambers. Some Yoomans *enjoy* tormenting cats."

"That's true enough," I said with a shudder, thinking of the gleeful way which Horrible had shoved me into his sack.

"Whatever it is they do to us, they try to catch us in the Van."

"Is it known where they take the cats they capture?" I asked quizzically. The dread of this Van had already begun to overcome me. Already I began to feel that unless we all stuck together, there would be no escape from the Van. And I felt this even though I had no idea what the Van was nor whither it took its victims.

About a week later, when I was out on the prowl with Twinkle, I actually *saw* the Van with my own eyes. We had crossed the patch of waste ground where we lived and were doing some routine dustbin work about an hour before daylight, at the back of a grocer's shop on the corner of a street.

"Mostly rubbish," said Twinkle, throwing down bins and cardboard. "But there is a broken egg here. Too messy to carry back. Why don't you eat it, brother?"

Our eyes met. I was very hungry and would dearly have loved to eat that egg. But I knew that if I did so while on the prowl, Twinkle would report me to Tom-Cat, and I should be sentenced to starvation punishment.

"All food belongs to Tom-Cat," I said solemnly.

"Brother Tom-Cat," said Twinkle. "I shall eat it if you don't."

I was unable to tell whether this, too, was a piece of double-bluff – whether Twinkle was tempting me to say disloyal things about Tom-Cat in order to have something to report back to my detriment or whether they were spontaneous outbursts of feeling. Anyhow, he wolfed the egg. He must have known that I was too recent an arrival in the Commune to risk denouncing *him* to the authorities. But just as he was eating the egg, he froze, and then quick as a flash, hissed, "Follow me!" In a split second he had climbed up a drain pipe, on to the top of a low-lying wall, and across on to a window ledge, where it was possible to be concealed in the shadows. I sat there beside him, my body tingling with the excitement of the chase, and yet at the same time, on the edge of a nameless fear. He made no sound, but with a slight inclination of the head, he indicated what was happening in the street below. Opposite the dustbins which we had been cleaning out, a pretty little Siamese cat was pawing her front door, demanding that a human slave should come and let her in. I could even hear her words – "Oh come *on* – you surely aren't asleep, you cretins!" And then, round the corner of the street, there came the Van. It was not a particularly large van, but it stopped, and a man got out of it. He wore big leather gloves, and a thick coat. He was well protected. Only by flying at his face with claws out would there have been any hope of resisting him. He simply stooped down and picked up the Siamese – and even as she was calling out – "Put me *down*, you barbarian!" he shoved her into a sack. He opened the back of the Van, threw in the sack, and shut the Van again. Then he got into the front of the Van where another man sat at the wheel. A few minutes later, an old lady who rather reminded me of Granny Harris, opened her door and called out, "Millicent! Millie, dear! Millie-Millie, Mill-i-cent!" She looked up and down the street with puzzlement. After that, I never doubted the existence of the Van. Nor could I find reason to doubt that no cat on its *own* could resist the Van. It was only within the safety of the Commune that one felt able to survive, thanks – yes, the claptrap began to enslave me – thanks to the valiance and courage of our great Brother Tom-Cat.

CHAPTER THIRTEEN

I am not very proud of the fact that, had life in the Commune gone on for much longer, I should probably have turned into one of old Tom's hench cats, bullying the others, and dreaming one day of superseding Tom-Cat as leader. Remembering the important way in which Jim, while addressing the yellow-shells, had not called himself Jim, but Regional Area Manager, I even dreamed of adopting this title myself when one day I became Chief of the Commune. Had this happened of course I would gradually have ceased to be feline. I would have become a terrible parody of the human world. But Fate spared me, and although I dreamed of power I never exercised it. I never challenged Tom-Cat's leadership, nor superseded it, nor gave myself the title of Regional Area Manager. Fate stepped in and brought the Commune to a terrible end.

None of us, I think, had suspected the possibility of such a thing for an instant. We had all come to believe quite firmly that the chief end of life was to escape the Van, and that the only means of escaping the Van was to huddle in that garage and accept the bullying regime of Brother Tom-Cat. As soon as one considers the matter rationally, one realizes what an absurd belief this was. I think we were more at risk in the Commune than any ordinary domestic cat with human minders such as your own. Think of the fuss they make if you go missing for more than a few hours! The Van-Man would have a lot of explaining to do if he bumped into your human slaves while he was shoving you in his bag; whereas, no one would complain if he picked up "common strays". Moreover, as I now realize, there was nothing safe about twenty or thirty cats all shutting themselves up in one garage. True, there were a few broken windows through which we could get in and out. But there was only one door, and any human being who commanded that door commanded the Commune.

This in fact was what happened. I suppose we shall never know how they found us. Perhaps they had followed some pair on the prowl. Perhaps they had just decided to check the garage for the odd stray. For whatever reason, the garage door opened one night, a torch was shone round, and in the next ten minutes, Tom-Cat's huge power was brought to an ignominious end.

The raid of the Van men took us wholly by surprise. We were all huddled in the garage all, that is, except the pair out on the prowl. Some of the kittens were asleep. A few of the fussier mothers were grooming their young, though however much they licked the puny, scabby little bodies of the kittens, they would not prevent them from being anything but mangy urchins. Other cats were pacing about in the dark, smelly garage. Tom-Cat himself sat on the window ledge and stared through the frosted glass at our great Mother-of-Night whose existence, in some moods, he denied. Then, all of a sudden, we heard the noise of an engine of murder outside. Probably it was no louder than most engines, but coming upon our midnight stillness so suddenly and unexpectedly, it sounded as loud as a thunderstorm or a falling dustbin lid. And we had no time to recover from the shock of the noise before the garage door was forced open and a torchlight was shone around us. I was momentarily blinded by its beam and blinked, while, from behind the beam there came an unpleasant human voice: "Blimey, there are dozens of the little beggars in here!"

"I'll get some more sacks," said another voice.

The mention of sacks was enough to make me want to escape. Were these some more men like Horrible who enjoyed throwing cats out of car windows when they were going along? Little did I suspect that these men were in fact

114

driving the Dreaded Van. I ran to the window ledge and said to Tom-Cat, "We've got to run."

"No cat leaves here without my permission," he snarled. I could see his eyes gleaming in the darkness and not for the first time I was struck by how deeply stupid he was.

"But they've got sacks," I said.

"What are sacks?"

"They'll put us in them and murder us," I said.

"It is only by staying in the Commune that a cat can escape the Van," said Tom-Cat flatly.

"That's true," said one of the hench cats, who started to call out, "Stay where you are, cats! Our great Brother Tom-Cat will protect you!"

But not everyone was obedient. Some of the younger cats stormed Tom-Cat's window-sill, knocked the leader to one side, and escaped into the night. They were the lucky ones. The Van driver and his friend had come back now. Not only were they clad in leather coats and gloves, but they even wore protective masks. And they were experts at their job. They picked up cats by the scruff of the neck and stuffed them into the sacks with as much ease as the pet shop man had shovelled rabbit food into paper bags. Tom-Cat himself was one of the easiest to catch. He had grown used to other cats doing everything for him. Perhaps he had even forgotten how to fight.

I hadn't. Nor had I forgotten how to hide. As the gruesome work proceeded, I darted out of the glare of the torchlight and hid in the shadows, watching. I reckoned that if I could get to the window ledge while the men were struggling to tie up their sacks, I would stand a pretty good chance of escape. But I mistimed it.

"This is a good bag," said one voice.

"Must be ten cats in each of these bags," said the other, "that's ten quid."

"If the laboratory will buy them all," said the first man. "Some of them looked pretty miserable specimens to me."

"They'll all be miserable specimens after a few weeks in the lab," said the second voice with a laugh. "I'm sure the lab will buy them. Scientists have a use for everything."

Probably these words "laboratory" and "scientist" mean as little to you now as they did to me then. I am still not able to explain to myself why these "scientists" behave as they do, but I do know *what* they do, as you shall hear. For I did not escape them. I leapt towards the window, but in the darkness I kicked against an upturned petrol can and made a terrific noise.

"There's another of the blighters," said first voice, and instantly turned his torch in my direction. Second voice was much nearer me than I had reckoned. I could not get to the window. I felt a heavy human hand on the back of my neck, and I was held up in the air like an exhibit, a specimen. That, as it happened, was what I was to be from now on.

"Oh yes, he's a beauty," said second voice. "Quite a big one. In you go." And everything went dark as I was shoved into the sack.

CHAPTER FOURTEEN

I do not like to remember the next period of my life. It is too disgusting. I thought in my most miserable days in the Commune, that I had sunk as low as it is possible for a cat to sink. But I was wrong. For the evils which a cat does to another can never match the immeasurable evil of which human beings are capable. You would be distressed to know all the sorrows which cats suffer in these "laboratory" places, so I will keep my story as brief as I can. I will not tell you of that terrifying journey in the sack, for every second of which I screamed my head off, certain that at any moment I would be thrown out of the Van window. We were all screaming and squirming on top of one another. There was no chance for a rational discussion of the situation, and what must have been the good of such a discussion if we had one? Our noble Leader was screaming as loud as the rest of us. I cannot say whether any of us *knew* that we were in the very Van which had been the object of all our fears. After quite a short journey the Van stopped, and we were left there in our sacks for what felt like a very long time. I suppose it was not more than a few hours. The next thing we knew, the sack was being lifted up, and we were being carried (as I later realized) indoors and up some stairs. Then the top of the bag was opened and we were shaken out. Instinct made me run for it. But there was no point. We were being emptied out into a cage.

First voice and second voice, from the night before, had gone now. I am happy to say that we never heard them again. But round our cage there stood a group of equally sinister men and women, all of whom wore white coats and some of whom had eye-glasses.

"A rum collection," remarked a woman peering at us. "I reckon we can only use half these. This for instance, wouldn't survive the course," and she picked up a small kitten. I felt immediate envy for that little cat because I naively supposed that, finding no use for him, the woman was about to release him. He was about your kind of age, little Grandkitten, but smaller and punier and a good deal dirtier because of the life he had been leading. You can imagine how I felt when I saw this woman wring his neck with her own hands and throw the little chap into a large plastic dustbin.

"The ones we keep will need fumigating," she said, "if they are as flea-ridden as that one."

You will be wondering where I was and what I was doing there. You might even be wondering *why* the human beings in white coats were behaving in this manner. I am afraid that I am unable to satisfy your curiosity. I do not know what the place was where they had taken me. And I think that, even by that stage of my life, I had given up asking why human beings behave as they do. As my brother and I would say, "Really – they are extraordinary!"

But their extraordinariness is not always comic. I have endured many a fight with my own kind. I have known the cruelty of foxes, and the savagery of dogs; but there is nothing to match the venomous cruelty of human beings.

The place of my imprisonment was the very "laboratory" of which Tom-Cat had taught us to be afraid. I had often heard the white-coated oafs refer to it as the "lab", a word they also seem to use sometimes for the well they sit on. After they had treated me for fleas, and decided that I was a "fine specimen", I was separated from my fellows and locked in a small cage. I will say this for the lab: they did not starve you. To that extent it was a good deal more comfortable than the pet shop. And although I hated being shut up in a small cage, I began to think that things might be worse. How right I was. For the second day, some

118

glistening human faces appeared at the bars of the cage and began to peer in at me.

A couple of white-coats were talking.

"Is that enough lipstick?" one was asking.

The other white-coat was making that horrible noise with his mouth which he called laughter.

"You can't help laughing when you see a cat with its mouth covered with lipstick," he said.

"I can," said the other white-coat. "In fact I think it's a horrible business."

"Oh come on now. Don't get all high and mighty!"

"I'm not. But I don't think that a laboratory like this should be wasting its time on lipstick, that's all."

"What does it matter what it wastes its time on? It's all research, isn't it?"

The nastier of the white-coats seemed to set a lot of value on searching for this ree. I have asked several cats as fluent in catching human speech as myself what ree is, but none has been able to tell me.

"Those cats in there are being smothered with lipstick just so that cosmetic firms can make money out of silly women," said the nicer white-coat.

"I suppose you'd rather we tested the lipsticks on people," said nasty. "Would you like your wife's lips to become like that poor moggy's mouth in there?"

"I don't want anyone's mouth to become like that: not my wife's, nor the cat's. There is no need to *have* lipstick, if it can only be got with suffering like this. Now if we were testing the animals for medical research, to help us cure terrible diseases, or something of that kind, I would understand it. But we aren't. That row of cages is lipstick. Over there, it is meant to be psychology, but we know perfectly well, we are just playing games with these animals. Look at those rats, smoking in there."

"Oh, cut it out, Gerry!" said nasty. "If you feel like this you shouldn't be working in a lab. Go and join the Animal

119

Rights nutters if you're so sorry for a lot of stupid animals."

"I've half a mind to do just that," said less nasty, and he walked away in anger. It was left to nasty to open the door to my cage and call out to another white-coat, "It's shampoos in here, isn't it?"

"I think so," said the other one.

"Go easy with the stuff," he added. "We don't want too many bald, blind cats on our hands. Remember the last lot?"

"Do I *not*?" laughed nasty, and he set to work. He got some soapy liquid out of a bottle and began to rub it into my fur in small patches. Then he locked me up again. At first this was not too bad, but after a while it began to itch and sting like crazy. And hour after hour, day after day, the brute came back with lots of little bottles and rubbed the stuff into my fur until at length I was stinging and sore all over. Nasty seemed interested in the "results". He entered them into some sort of chart or other with his pen, and after a few days, he exclaimed, "Well, it may cure dandruff, but it will bring you out in such sores, you'd wish you'd never used the stuff. Back to the drawing board."

He lifted me up. I thought I was for it, and I struggled. He took me over to a sink, and started to run the tap. I was sure that he was trying to drown me, and I scratched and fought for all I was worth.

He hit my face and told me to stop that game, but I was determined that it would take more than Nasty White-Coat and a sink full of water to bring me to the Great Stillness. But, oddly enough, he lowered me into the water and simply rinsed me until all the nasty soapy substance was removed from my fur. Then he rubbed me roughly with a towel, and took me back to the cage to dry off and gave me, I remember, quite a palatable bowl of mice to eat. But by then I knew enough not to imagine that the torture was ever finished. They might leave you alone for a few hours, or a few days, but they would always come back to torment you some more.

While I ate the mice, however, my ears pricked up. Nasty was talking to the other white-coat about the less nasty one called Gerry.

"Fancy old Gerry leaving us," said Nasty.

"I always did think Gerry was a bit bonkers," said the other.

"That's right. A bit of a loner, Gerry. Liked to make up his own mind on things," said Nasty.

"Like I say, a nutter."

"Did you hear about the letter he wrote to the local papers?"

"No?"

"Yes. The boss is livid. Furious. Says it's a breach of security, professional something or another. Furious the old man is. Gerry has written to the local papers saying that the existence of this laboratory is a scandal to the town. He says that we are cruel to animals."

"I always get bored when people go on about cruelty to animals," said the other white-coat. "As if there weren't enough suffering people in the world, without worrying about animals. Oh shut up!" he shouted, at a cage from which the most terrible screams were proceeding.

"Anyway. Old Gerry's taken my advice," said Nasty. "He says in this letter that he has joined the nutters."

"Not the Animal Rights Group."

"Right," said Nasty. "Said he would do all in his power to bring cruel experiments on animals to an end. Said the law should be changed. Said if necessary he'd break the law."

"And get past the security guards and the police, and the guard dogs. I don't see old Gerry doing that. Half the time he even forgot to hand in his key after work," said the other one.

"That's a thought," said Nasty. "I wonder if Gerry handed in his keys when he left us?"

It was not a question which interested me. I am completely baffled by the human taste for locks, and for shutting

121

things. Doors and windows are useful enough. But not if they are *shut*. I hear your human minders shouting at you and your mother sometimes, and I wonder how you put up with it. "Are you coming in or aren't you?" they call. "Oh don't just stand and hover by the door, make up your mind!" Well *hovering* is the most sensible thing to do by a door if it is the only way to stop some fool human from shutting it in your face.

These questions were far away in my cage. When I had dried out, and finished eating my mice, Nasty approached once more and started work with a different set of bottles. This time, instead of rubbing the soap in my back fur, he rubbed it on my head, and on my face. He even deliberately put soap in my eyes, and this process was repeated over the next fortnight with a dozen different bottles. When you are in pain, the whole world gets blotted out. All the sensations which are natural and joyful, all your awareness of the world itself is gone. Eating is no pleasure. Sleep is hardly possible. You can only think of the ache or the sting or the agony. And that was what it was like for me in that fortnight. I was in constant pain, and I felt powerless. And many a time in my agony, I came half to long for the Great Stillness, or, what was an almost equal condition of despair, to remember with a nostalgic sweetness, my days of safety when I was a slave of Tom-Cat's in the Commune.

CHAPTER FIFTEEN

But then, everything changed, quite suddenly.

While I was sitting in my cage, and thinking the blackest thoughts that a cat ever thought, and smarting in the eyes, and hating my captors with a weakness of hatred that only the victims of such cruelty would fully understand, there was a violently loud crash. Glass was being broken, a door was being battered down. There was a sound of human voices yelling and baying. My feelings of rage and desolation and despair sharpened into sensations of acute terror. The monsters in white coats were our enemy. That was for sure. But already, there was something half-reassuring in knowing them to be our enemy. Can you begin to understand this? We knew where we were with them. My hatred for them could not change. It will never change. And yet, between us there had grown up a relationship of mistrust which had such routines and boundaries and fixities that it was almost as reassuring as a relationship of trust! Hatred, like love, has its routines. The most terrible element in fear – uncertainty – had been absent in the previous weeks, days or whatever they were. Now, uncertainty entered in once again. Who was making such a din? Why? I came to the front of my cage and looked through the wire. I could see a curious vision. A man with fur growing from the bottom of his face, as well as sprouting from the top had entered the laboratory. He had very long fur, tied in a pigtail at the back: he had a bright red shirt and blue trousers and a wild look in his eyes. He was accompanied by a woman with short lank yellow fur growing on her head and she too was wild.

"I just can't believe it," she was saying.

123

"I can," said he. "I can believe it all too easily."

"I feel so – so angry," she said, with passionate intensity, "that I could do violence to them. I could really. I could tear them limb from limb."

Now, it did not occur to me that this wild woman was talking about our human tormentors. I thought she was talking about us, the tormented. I assumed that she was a madwoman who had burst into the laboratory with the intention of tearing me limb from limb, and I began to let out uncontrollable howls. Suddenly, life seemed very sweet; even life as hellish as the existence which my tormentors made me live in the laboratory. Better a life of having shampoo rubbed in my eyes morning and afternoon, than the Great Stillness.

"Look at that one," said the woman, "it's got such sore eyes. Yes, you," she said, suddenly looking at me and addressing me in tones of such tenderness that for a moment I thought of Granny Harris and Sister Caroline Mary. "You've got sore eyes."

Other people had come into the laboratory – men and women. One said, "We've let the monkeys out in the next room, and the rats. They're in boxes. We are carrying them out into the vans. But what about the cats?"

"They'll have to go too."

"Oh, my God!" the woman was screaming now. "Just look at this one. She was peering in the cage next to mine. Because it was next to mine I had not been able to see inside it, but she now opened the door of his cage and brought out my neighbour for her friends to see.

I still did not understand that these people were my friends. I mewed and miaowed furiously. I had heard my neighbour screaming all week; I did not know exactly what he had been through, but it seemed monstrous to me that he should have been tortured by the scientists, and had his life spared only to be tormented by these wild people.

But the woman was crying. Her eyes looked as red and sore as mine felt, and I could see her holding my poor

124

neighbour to her breast as though he had been one of her own babies. And then I knew that these people, strange as they looked and seemed and smelled, were our friends, and the dreadful fear which their entry into the laboratory had caused me changed to excitement and joy. But it was a joy very decidedly shot through with sorrow. For the sight of my neighbour, held up by that poor weeping woman was a shocking one.

The scientists had cut off his tail – presumably it got in the way of one of their infernal machines. And now I saw what he meant, as he cried out, day after day, "I cannot close my eyes! I cannot close my eyes." For they had cut off his eyelids. At first I could not make out what was strange about his eyes. I thought that they had just been smearing them with shampoo and making them sore, like mine. But he was not testing shampoo, he was testing "sleeplessness".

"They'd put him on a treadmill," sobbed the woman. "They'd strapped him on a treadmill and forced him to go on and on, without ... without any eyelids."

I could hardly recognize that animal which she held in her arms. He was so mutilated that there was almost nothing left of him. But in my memory of the sight of him, I become more and more certain that this poor creature was Tom-Cat himself.

"It's one of the most notorious experiments," said the man. "They are testing the effects of sleeplessness. We must hurry, we must get all the cats out. And the birds, and the mice. But we must be careful not to get them all out at once. It wouldn't be very kind to the mice or birds."

I cannot tell you how those words cheered me up. For they reminded me of the pleasures which I thought would be denied me for ever and ever: the pleasure of being free, and out in the open air; free to chase a bird or a mouse, free to run and hop and jump about. It had not been long, the period of my incarceration. By the measurements of men, I guess it would not have been two or three weeks. But already I had given up hope of ever leading a normal feline life again. Indeed, ever since I had left the Sisters, and become caught up in the "feral community", I had rather forgotten what normality was. But it was the man's joke about the hunt which brought my mind back to reality, and there stirred within me a passionate longing for the sun, for the air on my fur, for aloneness. No, it was not just a longing to be alone. It was a desire to be myself. Everything that had happened to me since my brother died had somehow or other contrived to stop me being myself. Yes, even in the happy days of recovery with the Sisters. And in that simple reflection of the man – that if I was let out of my cage I would want to chase the mice – there breathed an echo of that far-off country in which I had always been the citizen, but which I had never known or seen: that place whither, from my exile, one day I would be bound. Whether it was a place or a cat, I did not know.

It was the feeling that the old Major had awoken in me when he spoke of "taking to the road".

It is a longing for home, which now and here no home could satisfy: it is a permanent sense of exile. In it, I was looking forward to the alluring and unknown future, but in that looking forward, there was this element of a *return*, the feeling that one day, at last, I would be back in that state of perfect happiness with which I had begun to be conscious: that state before I even opened my eyes, in the back bedroom of some unknown house, that profound state of security and love.

Is that what I felt? Or just an eagerness to be away? I stood on my hind legs and clawed at the wire of the cage, calling out with anguished excitement. They were opening other cages before mine, and I wanted to be free! Why not come to me! To me! To me!

At each cage, one or other of the liberators themselves let out exclamations of horror at what they saw there. My friend and neighbour who had been mutilated in the "sleep" experiment was the worst off. But other cats there were in a terrible condition. Some poor devils who had been having the same shampoo treatment as myself had already gone blind, and staggered to and fro, uncertain of what was happening, calling out with anxiety. Were they free, as it felt? Or were they merely being led away to worse tortures and viler humiliations? Others could hardly cry out because their shaved fur had been smeared with the colouring with which some women paint their mouths. Only in this case, the colouring had been somehow poisoned, and their lips were swollen or cracked or deformed. Others – thin and limping – were losing their fur and stared out from bald scrubby heads like demented monkeys. It was the sorriest gang of cats that I ever saw in my life. A few of the younger kittens were frisky and started to run about the laboratory, and to do as the liberators feared: they had leapt up on to a shelf where mice and guinea-pigs were groaning in cages, and were callously thumping at the bars. Who could blame them? A young cat is a young cat, and acts on instinct. It was the other lot who were acting out of the normal. They allowed themselves to be herded like so many sheep, and directed into a neighbouring room.

"They're not going to survive, are they?" one of the women was saying sadly. "The kindest thing we could do to these animals is to kill them here and now. Look at this moggy. Oh, my poor pet!" And she picked up a thin, yelping balding wretch who was coughing badly. This woman and a helper were lifting the cats into large laundry baskets. Could it be that after all, these liberators were not our friends, but our enemies?

I did not propose to find out. In any case, I still had enough energy and enough curiosity to want to run around into the other rooms and shelves in the laboratory, and to see what the young kittens were seeing. So when my turn came to be liberated, I bounded through the door, biting the hand which freed me, and scratching with all claws out.

"He's a wild one, this."

"Has he bitten you, Sebastian?"

"It isn't serious."

But a glance behind revealed that there was blood pouring from the bearded man's hand, and the interest which this created gave me time to get out. Instinct told me not to linger in that place. I could see all I wanted to see, and more, without loafing around the cages as some of the young kittens were.

"Cor!" one of them was saying. "Look at that rat."

"It isn't a rat, it's a gerbil."

"Hello, darling! Like to come out with me!" called the cruel young cats to the terrified little creature in its cage.

"You'll never get through the door hammering like that."

"Oh, yeah! Well you try if you're so clever!"

"Cats!" I called. "It isn't worth staying there and quarrelling about a poor little animal in a cage. Probably if you ate it, it would poison you. We must get out."

"Pufftail's right," said one of the young blades.

"What did you say?" I hissed back. "I am a cat of no name. Remember that."

"They all call you Pufftail," said the cheeky young tom – a ginger, it was. "We've taken to doing the same. We've seen you, pacing up and down in your cage as if you were a lion or something."

"You can stay if you like," I said, "but I am going, and if you take my advice, you'll go too."

"'If you take my advice.'" The young kittens imitated my voice and then dissolved into merriment, but one or two saw the force of my suggestion, and scampered after me. In the next room, I froze on my feet with fear because I could smell the smell which only comes from human mouths – that peculiar smoke which emanates from the paper chimneys, an acrid, choking smell.

"Get back," I hissed to the two or three kittens who were following me. "Stand still. There's a man in here."

"How do you know?"

"I can smell the smoke."

For no reason at all, I assumed that the human liberators would not be the smoke-breathing sort of being. I realize

128

now that is a completely false piece of logic, but at the time smoke meant to me only one thing: a human enemy — Bob and his friend in the car — cruel oafs!

"I can't see a man," said one of the young kittens.

"Nor I," said his friend. "It isn't a man who is smoke breathing. It's the rats in that cage. Look!"

You know he was right! For all my policy of not lingering in my desire to get out of that hell hole of a laboratory as fast as my legs would carry me, I stood transfixed by the sight which the young ginger tom indicated with his paw. For there, in a long cage on a table ledge against the wall, were about twenty rats jostling with one another to suck cigarette smoke from a tube.

"'Ere, rat, give us a suck."

"'E's always pushing, that rat is, rat."

"I don't push rat no more than you does, rat."

"Oooh! oooh! ooooooh!" squeaked the satisfied rats who had their mouths round the tube. They were white rats with red eyes. About six tubes were fed from some sort of tank through a hole in the wall of their cage. Some machine or other was puffing smoke through these tubes, and far from being disgusted, the rats were loving it.

The rats called this puffing "having a drag".

"Oooh, rat, nice to have a drag, rat."

"Loooovely. I loves me drag."

Others in the queue were alternating between a desperate longing for a puff on the tube, and a desire to show the others that they did not really mind whether they puffed the tube or not.

"I just queue up for the company, rat. Tell the truth, I don't care whether I haves a drag or not, rat."

"If that's true, rat, why push ahead, rat?"

"Push, rat? Me rat? No, but fair's fair. If we're all entitled to a drag, rat, I'll have my fair share. But no, it makes no difference to me whether I drag or not."

"You only had a drag five minutes ago, rat."

"Hurry up, rat in front there. I wants a drag."

They had no interest in anything except this smoke, which came in regular little puffs down the tube. Then, it stopped. Clearly, the tubes were programmed, so that they puffed smoke for half an hour, and then stopped doing so. After only a very few minutes, the rats' whole demeanour changed. They began to quarrel in earnest, even to fight and scratch one another. At the same time, they staggered to and fro, coughing and belching and only half able to breathe.

The sight both fascinated and disgusted me, but after a little while, I was overcome with that feeling of weak hatred for the human race which had so often afflicted me since coming to the laboratory. I have never thought of myself as a great defender of the rat, either as a species or as an individual. But there is a world of difference between a rat leading its own ratty life (repulsive as that may be) and the sight of these creatures, who had stopped being rats, and had not become anything else, mere creatures of desire, and an artificial desire at that, manipulated and set up by men in white coats.

"Let's go, Pufftail," said one of the cheeky young kittens, and for once I felt no desire to cuff him or put him in his place. We all felt the same – shocked, and angry and dizzy with it all. Outside the rat laboratory, there was a stone staircase, I had not realized that we were upstairs before. But as we ran down it, we saw that men in blue uniforms were coming through the doors at the bottom of the stairs.

"They smashed all the glass, sir," said one of the men in blue.

"Not just that, Sergeant. Look at that." And with a stubby finger, the senior man in blue was pointing at me. "They must have opened the door into the lab. What beats me is how they picked those locks. Now they'll have cats and rats and monkeys all over the place."

"They surely wouldn't be so irresponsible as to let out all the animals," said the man whose name was Sergeant. "I mean, they'll have diseases and such. Don't touch that one there, sir. I advise you not to touch it."

130

Yes, "it". And they were still speaking of me!

"But this is anarchy," another of the men in blue was saying. "We've got the building surrounded with men and dogs who should pick up any of the maniacs who started all this nonsense. Cor! Did you see that plate glass door? Just smashed!"

"They're mad!"

"They think they are on the side of the animals, and they claim that they're stopping animals from being tortured, but they are just maniacs. That's all they are."

"What about the strays they're letting loose, sir?" asked Sergeant.

Sir said, "If we can't stop them with the dogs we shall have to shoot them. They'll all have to be put down anyway. Criminal's the word I'd use. When you think of all the good that a place like this has done to the human race. I mean, without science, quite frankly, where would we be? Back in the Middle Ages, I shouldn't wonder."

I still do not understand what happened. That is, the whole episode of my time in the laboratory is incomprehensible to me. Obviously, by torturing us in our cages, the white-coats were pretending that they were finding out some very important secrets. Whether they believed this themselves, or whether it was just a trick they were playing on the stupider people, such as Sergeant and Sir, I will never know. But then there was this other group of people, the man with beard fluff, and the lank woman who wept, who were the enemies of the white-coats and the blue-uniforms. And they, it seemed, had come to rescue us. But out of pity, love of animals, or simply out of hatred for the white-coats? What were they planning to do when they put the cats in the basket or let the pigeons out of their cages? We shall never know, because the blue-uniforms arrived to stop them.

"We'll never get out now," said one of the kittens to me quietly. "Did you hear that Sergeant person? Dogs, and if we get past the dogs they'll shoot us."

"We've got to get out," I said.

131

"That's just talk," said the ginger tom. "I'd rather sit in the cage all day than be torn to pieces by a dog. Besides, I was almost getting used to it."

"That is precisely why we must escape," I said. "Did you *see* those rats upstairs? Did you not see what the white-co had done to them? They had done something much worse than deliver them to the Great Stillness. They had allowed them their breath but made them use that breath only for puffing smoke. They had allowed them their movement and vigour. But every ounce of energy which those silly creatures had left was devoted to filling their lungs with that horrible smell. They had allowed them existence, but they had created a mockery of it by changing the very essence of that existence. They had stopped the rats being themselves. Now a cat who says he is happy to be in a cage and is getting used to having soap rubbed in his eyes is little by little ceasing to be a cat. Don't you see it would be better a thousand times to run out there and risk meeting a dog, than to creep upstairs again into your cage? Don't you know that it has always been our destiny to battle with dogs, and to fight against destiny? And though to be oneself brings sorrow and grief, and though it leads to the Great Stillness itself, there is still no other path that a self-respecting cat can follow."

Thus I spoke — or words to that effect. Evidently I won my point, for all three kittens with me recognized that we had no choice. We had to make a dash for it. The trouble was that we had absolutely no sense of the terrain. We had been brought here in bags. We had been imprisoned in cages. Our glimpse — beyond the door, was of sunlight falling onto a drive, some lawn, a wall. But what was beyond?

"Each for his own," I said. "And remember — no dog can climb a wall."

"Pufftail," said the ginger tom who had up to this point been preaching doctrines of cowardice. "Thank you. You have saved me."

132

"Only your own will and the swiftness of your feet can save you now," I said.

"You know what I mean," he said. And of course I did.

He sprinted out ahead of us across the grass, and almost at once the uniformed men let loose two enormous dogs the size of wolves: the breed called by men Alsatians. The two great monsters bore down upon the young ginger cat, but just before they reached him, they paused, much as we would pause before going into the kill when hunting a vole or a mouse.

I ran into the yard, too, and so did the other pair of kittens.

"I've got them interested!" shouted ginger to us. "Run now, while you can!"

"But..." I called.

"No buts," he called back. "You were right! Thank you, Pufftail! For I was about to lose my soul, and now I have found it again."

At this stage, the dogs – who of course did not understand our speech and only heard what they thought were squeaks and miaows, let out that frightening roar which they make, "Raw! raw! raw! raw!" and they fell on our young friend.

I ran, faster than I have ever run in my life, and with a magnificent bound, I managed to scale the top of the wall. So did two of my companions. But they got a third, as well as the ginger. Neither cat could struggle for long. Looking back across the scrub of grass, I saw the dogs gnawing still little bundles of cat-fur. There was blood on their mouths.

So this was the glory, and this was the soul, unto which I had called him! But he was right, of course, and I had been right, and it was better to sleep at the hands of a dog than to live at the hands of a cruel man.

Beyond the wall, there were men with cameras, and a little huddle of people, but oddly enough they were all looking towards the gates. They ignored us. They snapped the cameras when the uniform men dragged the man with

133

beard fluff and his friends into the backs of vans. But we were ignored, and we all ran as fast as we could down a pavement, through some railings, over what seemed like a park, and into some bushes for shelter.

"Now," I said, "I believe that we are free once more. And we must all go our own way."

CHAPTER SIXTEEN

I ran and ran and ran. There had been times when I ran before, as on the fateful night when I made my farewell to Sister Caroline Mary. Then I had run heedlessly. Now I did so warily, conscious, as I have been ever since, that every step you take in this world might be a step towards slavery or unhappiness. But even this knowledge, which has by now become second nature to me, could not stop floods of joy bathing over me as I ran through the fields and ditches, leaving the nightmare laboratory and the sound of human voices far behind me.

I was free! The wind was in my fur. The great sky was above my head. And for the first time in months, the world was all before me. The sensation of escape was in itself exciting enough: of knowing that I had left the dogs and the guns behind me. But this positive sense of freedom was even better. For weeks, I had been a prisoner in a laboratory, penned into a tiny cage, with nowhere to stretch my limbs. Before that, I had passed what now seemed an eternity, penned up in that garage as a member of Tom-Cat's Commune, and only allowed out "on the prowl" in my capacity as a food collector for the other cats. Before that, there had been my spell in the sick bay with the Sisters, and before that, the dreadful domestic life of Jim and June. It was long since I had tasted true freedom. Therefore, though I ran warily, I ran hard, anxious to put as far as possible between myself and my tormentors, and certain that from now onwards, I would let nothing and no one trick me into captivity. Never again. The next time, I would rather choose the Great Stillness, and that is still my resolution.

At one point in my run, I badly miscalculated, and came

135

to a barbed-wire fence. I saw that in my haste I had run through a field of sheep, almost without noticing them! And now, beyond the barbed-wire, I saw chickens, barns and houses. I heard a dog barking. And then I saw it: a great black and white brute, standing in the muddy yard. He was, I should guess, about a hundred yards away from me. But he had seen me all right, and was letting out his crude Ra-ra-ra to inform everyone else, should they be interested, that I was on the scene. The sheep did not seem to care much. But the dog's shouts alerted the notice of a greasy red woman, with her head tied in a cloth, who came out of the house and stared around the yard with unobservant stupidity.

"What be you a-barking at?" she asked. "There baint no dog among the sheep, be there?"

"Ra-ra-ra!" which I imagine, if dogs were capable of polite speech as we are, would have been rendered, "Madam, there is a cat among the sheep and I would dearly love to chase it!"

"Oi can't see nothin'," said the greasy woman. And then she did see me. "Well, bless me, what be that in the sheep field. Wal'er! Wal'er!"

"Ar?"

A male came out of the house. His legs were tied up with string, and he had an old cloth cap on his head.

"What be that animal with the sheep?"

"What animal?" asked Walter scornfully. "I don't see no animal."

"Ra-ra-raaa!" By now the dog had run to the edge of the field and was only forty or fifty yards away from me. He yapped and howled through the barbed-wire, and then ran to the gate which he pawed and sniffed, anxious to be let into the field to chase me. I was by now feeling pretty tired from my run, and could have done without this particular form of afternoon sport.

"That grey thing!" persisted Greasy. "Looks almost like a badger to me."

"Oi remember years ago how a badger *did* get one of my grandfather's sheep. But years ago, mind. Oi still don't see no badger."

I did not stay for the rest of this fascinating conversation, but I could not help overhearing the following snatches.

"Ain't you got eyes, Wallerollerton? You'd see better if you wore them glarrrsiz and drank less of that whisky. There be an animal in that field, else whattud Patch be a barrrkinat? And it's moi belief it's a woild cat."

"Now a woild cat could kill a lamb," said old Walter Hollerton slowly.

"Oh moind owta moi way, Wallerollerton and oi'll let Patch into the field. He'll be able to sort out what from what even if you baint."

And this the redoubtable lady proceeded to do. I wasn't looking, but I could hear the gate being swung to, and I knew that a young dog with months of training behind him was being set upon an extremely tired cat. I had a couple of hundred yards start on him, but I was aware that at any moment, my legs would simply give way to exhaustion. The barking behind my ears was getting louder and closer. A quick, and very scared glance over my shoulder told me that the dog was fast on my heels. It was touch and go whether or not he would catch up with me by the time I reached the next fence. And if he did catch me up, I did not greatly look forward to our encounter. But I made it. Just. And by the stile in the corner of that field, there was a sturdy oak, with low spreading branches and thick foliage. Even in my frail, tired condition, it was the work of a moment to jump up into the tree and hide in the branches. My whole body shook with exhaustion. My heart was palpitating, my legs were shaking, my very eyeballs were throbbing, when a couple of seconds later, the dog reached the bottom of the oak, and looked up at me hungrily. Had Walter Hollerton followed the dog with his gun, they might both have had sport of me that day. But the lazy old man had not so much as toddled out of his farmyard, and it was left to Patch to

137

stand at the roots of the tree and bark. I could now see that he was a clever dog, with sharp intelligent eyes and – now that I was safe from his jaws, even I could see that he had rather a pleasant face. He shouted and barked a bit more, but he knew the game was up and that I had won. He was soon scampering off across the field, through the first hedge and into the sheep field. Later that day, doubtless, he had work to do.

It is the thing about dogs which causes me most dread, this capacity of theirs for *work*. Yes, of course I fear their teeth and their anger and their rough love of sport at our expense. But most of all I dread that within them which is perfectly happy to be subservient to human kind. Why? What primeval curse have they inherited, what first terrible canine blunder took place, that they should be such cheerful slaves of a race lower than themselves? If the dog could drive the sheep, then, like enough, he could run the whole farm, and make the Hollertons do *his* bidding, instead of the other way about! But he did not do so. He served them, and served them with that pathetic happiness on his face which one so often distinguishes in dogs. The puzzle took hold of me as I sat there in the comforting branches of the oak, but it mingled in my brain with other thoughts. Recent memories of the laboratory and of that day's adventures pressed in at first, and then began to fade. I was a much younger, and more energetic cat, and a happier cat, as I settled deeper into sleep. My brother was with me once more. We were hunting in the back garden of Granny Harris's house. And I could see the Major, and hear him saying "Take to the road, take to the road..."

When I woke up, the dawn was just rising and the tree in whose thick branches I had found so comfortable a bed, was all a twitter with the song of birds. One of the many odd things about the lifestyle of human kind is the absolute *deadness* of everything they eat. Whereas for us, the natural thing is to eat things when they are more or less still alive – and at least, still warm. The human race – when it does eat flesh – disguises it by hanging and cooking and covering with gravy, so that half the joy of eating is removed. Most of the time, of course, they only eat flesh in *bits*, surrounded by such extraordinary ideas as sliced potatoes, beans in red sauce, pastry, or boiled vegetables. You can tell how much excitement there is in eating this sort of stuff if you look at their faces as they shovel it all in with knives and forks. You, young kitten, can imagine what it was like waking up to a dawn chorus of birds. But to explain that music to a human being you would have to ask him to imagine what it was like to wake up to a beautiful choir, and then to realize that the music emanated from a group of singing fried eggs or harmonious lamb chops. That is, the music was immediately and inextricably mixed up with my knowledge that it was coming from the throats of my breakfast. Stretching myself in the branches of the tree, and surveying the land below, I saw that there were no dogs or foxes or men in sight. At first I was lazy and greedy, and tried to catch a green woodpecker which happened to be nesting near my leafy hammock. This abortive lurch caused every bird in the tree to fly into the air squawking with horror, so I slithered down the trunk and lay low for ten minutes. Birds are wonderfully forgetful creatures and, like the rest of us, they get hungry. It was not long before I saw a plover straying from the middle of the field incautiously near my "hide". Its capture was the work of moments, and I was so hungry that I did not trouble to tease it and frighten it to death in the manner which gave my brother so much pleasure.

Hunger satisfied, I set off around the edge of the field, which was heavy with golden rye. The sun was just up; the air was pure, and the field and hedgerow were alive with tempting morsels. It was during that walk that I really developed my taste for field mice. And the hunting was so plentiful, and my new-found liberty so invigorating, that I decided to stay in those regions until something happened which would make me move along. I was a couple of weeks

139

there, I think, before men came in machines and mowed down all the corn. They were days of unalloyed happiness. And with each day that passed, I felt myself growing stronger in limb and clearer in my mind. I knew now that I was on the road, and I intended to remain as a free wanderer for the rest of my days.

It was the harvest which made me move on. I realized that nothing lasts for ever. But I was too happy to give myself up to contemplating exactly how human beings would choose to spoil that particular little paradise. I merely enjoyed it all while I could: my shelter in the old tree, and the cornfield so thick with life and food, and the long warm quiet hours, when there was no noise louder than the song of the birds and the whirring of crickets. And then, one morning, quite suddenly, it was all the roar of machinery and the shout of men. The roaring began on the other side of the field, and I saw a huge red engine, as large as a house, moving slowly up and down in rows, cutting down all the waving golden rye. I had just eaten my second field mouse of the day when the noise began, and I did not stay until the men with their machines reached my side of the field. It is astonishing to think how much food, in terms of mice, plovers, voles, rats, larks and stoats, gets *wasted* every year by this human habit of cutting down corn. But that is another story.

I was on my way and set off on the opposite side of the hedge at a brisk trot. A couple of fields beyond, there was a path between two hedges, at the end of which one could make out all the signs of human habitation: lamp posts, a pavement, a tarmac road with engines of murder driving up and down it; neatly trimmed grass, and brick houses which at first put me much in mind of Jim and June. Indeed, for one nasty moment, I thought it really *was* Jim and June's house. But it wasn't. I had stumbled upon a much more varied neighbourhood than Jim and June's estate. There were new houses like theirs, it is true; but also a lot of reassuringly messy old ones, plenty of filthy out-houses alive with rats, and garden sheds with mice and voles in them. This was no bad place to settle. Not for ever of course. I would never settle for ever. But for the time being.

CHAPTER SEVENTEEN

One autumn evening, long before the hour when human beings go to sleep, and leave the world to us and our great Mother-of-Night, I happened to be inspecting some dustbins and making some highly satisfactory discoveries. The dustbins were in a dark shady spot at the bottom of a garden and I could work undisturbed. The lid was one of those light plastic ones which you can lift off with a flick of the paw; and lying on top of the bin was a half-eaten duck! This really was a find: particularly since I had not, for some reason, eaten much that day. I decided to take the bird between my jaws, and to enjoy it in one of my accustomed hiding-places, on top of a nearby shed built against a wall. Not only could I sit on top of this roof and remain unmolested by people, foxes and other nuisances, but also I could be hidden even from cats, for it was a roof much overgrown with creeper. Eating my dinner in that spot was as good as being in some curtained chamber. On that misty night it was out of the cold and damp. I was just beginning to enjoy the duck when, two or three gardens away, I heard the yapping of a small dog. Normally, such a noise would have made less impression on me than the soughing of the wind in the trees. But for some reason – or perhaps for no particular reason – that evening I stopped, and listened. As well as yapping, there was a miaowing. One of our own kind – a female by the sound of it – was having trouble with the dog, and was calling for help.

Let her fight her own battles, I said to myself, as I savoured a particularly toothsome, fatty duck's wing. My days of being chivalrous are over. My days of wishing to impress females are over – females are to be had so easily any week of the year, without my trying to *impress* them. My days of taking risks are over. I wish to live only for myself and...

"Yap, yap, yap!"

"Help!" called the female voice. "Oh dog – do go away! Someone! Help!"

It was a confoundedly beautiful, attractive voice. But even then, as I tried to ignore it and to concentrate on my duck supper, I knew that there was something more *to* it, than to all the other female voices who had, at various stages of my history, sung alluring songs to me in the darkness. Nor was I deceiving myself when I said that the conquest of such sirens was easy. I had had many a mate, pursued her for a few hours or a few days and then forgotten about her.

And if I chased away the dog I would be able to enjoy *this* little beauty too... No! Why not simply enjoy my duck and avoid getting involved?

"Help! Oh, someone! Please help!"

I could not know what lay in store. Could I? And yet it was almost as if, in the very first few seconds of hearing her voice, I had an inkling of everything that was about to happen. As she called out "Someone! Please help!" I had the completely irrational response – What? Someone? Coming to *her* rescue? I couldn't tolerate it if just *anyone* presumed to lay a paw on *her*. She is *my* responsibility.

And I found that without thinking about it, I had dropped the duck into the hidden recesses of the foliage on the shed roof and set off over the garden fences in the direction of the yapping and the miaowing. Since my younger days, what a wary suspicious cat I had become. When my brother was still alive and we were lodgers at Granny Harris's house, I would have bounded along in the darkness without a thought of the dangers which shadows might contain. Such bravado was a thing of the past. I ran stealthily, aware that any summons for help might be a trap, and that even a fellow cat might be some communard on the prowl. But it was not long before I came upon the pair who were making all the noise. A King Charles's spaniel, only a shade larger than myself, had got a cat into a garden corner, and was bullying her. I could not make out her features. She was buried in shadow. I could only see the strutting overconfident figure of the spaniel, who had not even the presence of mind to bite his victim, but who was just standing there shouting and throwing his weight about. He was not a very observant dog. He did not see me looking down on the scene from the fence above his head. And when I pounced, I took him completely by surprise. I jumped on to his back, sinking my claws deep into his shoulder blades and biting the back of his neck. He yowled with pain and tried to roll over on his back. But this merely gave me the opportunity to scratch his face. He tried to bite me, but I was much too quick for him and after some notional growling, he limped off, calling no doubt for the protection of his human owners. They, probably, would soon be drooling over him and wondering who could have done such nasty scratches on their darling diddums. They would probably blame an Alsatian.

I was not interested in the spaniel's fate, but I was very interested indeed in whoever it was that sat hidden in the shadows.

"You seem to have annoyed that spaniel rather a lot," I said, speaking into the darkness and still unable to see anyone.

"They are easily annoyed," she said with a laugh. "There are two of them next door. It was silly of me to be scared, I know there is no harm in them really. But how thankful I am – that *you* came to the rescue!" And there was great emphasis on the word *you*.

She stepped out of the darkness and, on the half-lit path from the varied lights of a street lamp and uncurtained windows at the backs of houses, I saw her. She was a small grey tabby cat ribbed with delicate tiger-stripes all over her back and tail. Her chest was perfectly white, and her face was a mixture of tabby and white in all the right places. There is no point in telling you that she was the most

144

beautiful cat in the world, for you could probably find a thousand cats whose looks by some standard or another were more perfect. But ... she was the cat for me. I felt – no, I *knew* – as soon as I saw her that she was the cat I had been waiting for all my life. In fact, although I had not realized it until then, the whole of my previous life seemed as if it were nothing but a preparation for that moment.

"You look hungry," I said, "shaken..."

"They'll feed me," she said – and there was great tenderness about the next phrase – "when I get in" – because although she only *said* those four syllables, I *heard* much more. I heard, When I get in – but *please*, let us spend more time together before I go back indoors. Let us spend a *life* together...

"Would a bit of duck tempt you?" I asked.

"*Duck*?" she laughed.

"Yes! Come on!"

And side by side and happily we trotted back to my darkened shed-top retreat. Words cannot describe the hours which followed, the days and nights which followed. It would be foolish to try to describe them in all their innerness and secrecy. They were times which only two beings can share with one another and into which a third cannot enter. Suffice it to say that we were in love.

She lived, my beloved tabby, in a lodging house occupied by a number of human creatures all of whom, by the low standards of that race, were pretty decent. They were what is known as "animal lovers". In that household of three or four women and two men, there were, I should say, twelve cats, as well as all kinds of rats, mice, guinea-pigs, rabbits and what not. My particular beloved shared a room with a kind young woman, two other cats, and a cage of white rats. She described herself – and this caused me dreadful torments at first – as "very happy" in that house.

"Or at least," she said one evening, nestling against me, and licking my face, "I thought I was happy."

"I just hate to think of you in that house," I said, "being treated as a *pet*!"

"It is better than being treated as you have been treated," she said. For by then, she knew the story of my life.

"I know your present human minders are kind and decent," I said. "That isn't the point. Granny Harris was benign and decent and then, look what happened to her."

"That is something which happens to all living things," said my beloved.

Now, I had never heard anyone say that before, and I was so shocked that I sprang free from her and shouted, "No! That isn't true! Who *told* you such a thing? It happened to my brother – but the Great Stillness was brought upon him by cruel men. It happened to Granny Harris, it is true. But why it happened, I shall never know."

"My poor darling," she laughed. "You seem so wise and experienced, and so full of knowledge about the world. And had it never occurred to you that the Great Stillness, as you call it, is something which befalls *all* creatures? One minute, a bird dances and sings on its branch. The next it swoops down to get a worm from the lawn and *wham!* We eat it. But if we never ate it, the bird would still *die*; and so will the tree; and so will the lawn. All things are moving towards death. All things, that is, beneath our great Mother-of-Night. And who knows, perhaps the Great Stillness will one day come even upon her, and the earth itself."

"This cannot be!" I said. "For if it were true . . . why, the whole world would be nothing but a pile of rotting meat and dead bodies, and decayed flowers and dry grass, and leafless trees . . ."

"Nature always renews herself," she said. "We pass through it, but we give birth to new young. The flower withers and fades, the tree loses its leaves, but in a new year, there are new leaves, new grasses, new kittens. The old passes away. You must know that."

"No! No! No!"

I was utterly shaken that anyone could hold this point of

view, and I am completely sure that it is not true. It must be some wicked human idea that my poor beloved had picked up from the household where she lived. She said that it was the shortness of our lives which lent such sweetness to being in love. But I still believe that, with caution, we can all avoid the Great Stillness.

After she had told me her idea – that *we all die* – I felt overcome by a terrible fear, and by a deep sadness. It was not really *bearable* that the One I loved should think in this way. And yet, as I clung to her for comfort, I almost, on that dark evening, believed her. The Great Mother in the sky, instead of being a protectress and a governor of our destiny, seemed to smile upon us with indifference. And then it seemed as if we were just two beings surrounded by a great black nothingness: that the darkness of the night was the only reality; and that the only light which could ever penetrate it was not the beams of our Great Mother, but the love of our own hearts; and that the only weapon which we possessed against the Great Stillness was the knowledge that we too could renew ourselves, like the grass, and the trees and the flowers.

CHAPTER EIGHTEEN

You will have heard human beings up and down this street refer to my beloved as Tammy – just as they have that ridiculous "Pufftail" nonsense for me. But I hardly need stress that we did not have names for each other. We did not *need* names. She was (and is, and always will be) *She*. There can never, quite, be another She in the world. And I think I was the only *He* in her heart. I longed for her and me to take to the road, and to live quite independently of the idiot human race. And I think that she came to share my longing. That I really do believe. But she also wanted, in the very depth of herself, to have kittens. When I learnt that kittens were "on the way", I realized that our flight would be delayed until they were born. My darling wanted them to be safely born and kindly cared for, and she trusted her present human friends to look after that for her.

"Just be a little patient," she said. "When they are born and weaned, and can look after themselves – *then* we can go away together, and take to the road."

"And be together for ever and ever?" I said.

"And be together for ever and ever."

"And no more talk about *everybody* dying?"

She kissed me and hit my nose gently with her paw. "Oh, you poor simpleton," she said.

I think it fairly probable that I have been the father of over a hundred cats, and although I had sometimes taken pride in my offspring, when I knew they existed, they had never been of much interest to me. But I was desperately anxious that my darling should have a safe delivery. Moreover, for the first time in my life, I minded about the kittens themselves; I was aware, as I had never been before, that these beings, when they appeared, would be the products of our love. And I fell to thinking about my own mother, and those wonderful days before any human being intruded into our nursery, and it was just her, and my brothers and my sister and me, snuggling in warmth. In the bleak hostile world which mine had become, it once more seemed possible to re-create some of that warmth, some of that love.

"I'm still doubtful whether you are safe in that house," I said to my dear one day.

"Nowhere could be safer! Really, you are *funny* sometimes!"

"It's natural to be anxious."

"I've already told you – everything will be all right."

We were having this conversation on the same shed roof where we had had our first midnight duck-feast. Now it was a cold winter's day and it was broad daylight.

"I don't like all the other – *cats* in the house," I blurted it out with some awkwardness.

"I do believe you are jealous!" she laughed.

"Rubbish! I? Jealous? I merely think it is rather dreadful that you should have to share a house with – with that sort of riff-raff, that's all."

"Darling!" she laughed. "None of the cats can do me any *harm!* They are all just friends, and some of them aren't even that."

"Are you sure?"

"Of course! How can you doubt me?"

"I don't doubt you. I suppose I just don't like you being with anyone except me."

"That's silly."

"I know. I still can't help it."

"Tammy! Tammy!" At that moment, I could hear her human minder's voice, two gardens down, calling for her.

"Sounds as though it's dinner time," she said. She had a way of looking at you which was really rather mocking; and yet there was complete kindness, complete trustfulness in

149

the smile. It seemed to combine all cleverness with all love. "I'll walk half-way with you," I said.

"Don't try and come in with me or there'll be a fight with Bundle," she said. Bundle was the name given to a pretty little black and white female who lived in the basement below Tammy. "She always thinks you're coming in to get her food."

"A ridiculous misapprehension. As if I would!"

"As if you ever ate anything but someone else's food!"

"I, my dear? You mistake me. The idiot human beings tell their children stories of a man whom they call Robin of Greenwood. He robs the rich in order to give to the poor; and the children sing songs about him, and read books which perpetuate his name. Now I should not be surprised if in cat generations to come, they are not singing of the exploits of myself. What do I do except rob the rich – such as the poor old Major or your Bundle – in order to feed the poor. You cannot deny it."

"And the poor in this case?" she asked laughing.

"Very deserving in this case."

"Happens to be you," she said.

We walked along the crumbling brick top of the wall to the front of the house, and came to the pillar of yellow brick which served as a gate-post – though it was long since there had been a gate on that particular ramshackle residence. I looked up and down the street. It was by no means a bad place for a cat to have fetched up, if the notion of residence was one which stubbornly refused to be discarded. Further up, rows of two-storeyed terraced houses faced one another up and down the street. Down at our end, the houses were high cliffs of yellow brick, four storeys in height, soaring into the sky. There was a tree or two to relieve the monotony – handy when avoiding dogs. And up and down the backs of the houses, there were gardens, which themselves backing onto one another, made a vast area for us cats to explore. Here were more trees for climbing and resort; flower beds for lavatory accommodation; bird tables, where foolish sparrows, tits, thrushes and starlings would swoop – so eager for crumbs and bacon rind that they ignored one's approach. Here too were an abundance of the softer hearted type of human beings: the kind they call "cat lovers", so not all food had to be stolen. On the contrary, even though I had only been hovering about in that street for about a month, I already had my "regulars" who fed me. At Number Twelve, for example, they really do feed you awfully well. There are a couple of cats there – foreign names, black things, getting overweight – well, they've had the Operation, if you know what I mean – blow me, if they haven't persuaded their human slaves to put out a separate plate for *me* now and again.

The only trouble is, they will go in for this Pufftail nonsense. "Good evening, Pufftail." I eat my dinner and take no notice. But you *know* all this. I only tell it to you now because, at that midday parting with my darling, the street had a particular sweetness and beauty in my eyes, and I began to feel a yearning which was quite different from my original desire to "take to the road". I began to long for stability, warmth, assurance. I began to long for home. I was homesick, without knowing where on earth "home" was or might be.

She reached up and stroked my face with her paw. "What are you thinking behind those sad eyes?" she asked.

Her eyes, two great bright green leaves of light shone back at me.

"I was just thinking," I said, "how nice it would be if..."

"How nice what would be?"

"Well, it isn't the sort of thing I usually say, but..."

"Go on," she laughed at me, and we rubbed noses.

"I was just thinking how nice it would be if we were alone together and yet *secure*. At home, if you know what I mean. I was thinking how nice it would be – when the kittens are born – if we were both together in some warm spot, so that if I looked up, you were always there, and if you looked up, I was always there."

"What a nice thing to say."

"An even nicer thing to wish."

"Let's wish it then," she said. "Oh, I'm *coming*," she replied crossly as her young woman cried out "Tammy!"

"There she is, on the wall with Pufftail," said another human voice, this time of quite a young girl, a child really. "Are they fighting or what?"

"They aren't fighting!" laughed Tammy's minder. "They're always together these days. Tammy, people'll start talking about you if you don't come in for your dinner."

"It's tuna today," murmured my beloved. "I'll try and save you some. The trouble is, Bundle comes and eats it up if I leave any in the dish."

"I'll go round and see if they're opening a tin at Number Twelve," I said. "See you! This afternoon!"

But I didn't. As it happened, they had opened a modest tin at Number Twelve, and when I had eaten some of it I came outside and sat on the wall waiting for my darling to reappear from Number Eighteen. But she never came. I sat about for a bit. Then I paced up and down in the garden outside "her" house. But still there was no sign of her. And by the time darkness fell, I had begun to think very sad thoughts indeed.

I can hardly bear to recall that these thoughts really passed through my mind, but they did. In those hours, I came to *doubt* my beloved. Why had she promised to come back to me after dinner and then not reappeared? If she had really loved me, she would have come. And then the absurdity of my position began to strike me. Love! What did I mean by the word? I meant this aching desire to see her, this painful adoration. Had she ever shown signs of feeling such pain, or such worship? Had not her manner to me always been oblique, jokey, a little strange? Probably, I thought bitterly, she had always regarded me as an old fool; an old fool, moreover, who was also rather embarrassing, a bit of a bore. As I have said to you a hundred times, there had been lots of other female cats in my life and I had never

152

felt like this about any of them. What reason was there to suppose that *She* felt like this about me? Probably at this moment, she was sitting in Number Eighteen with her friends and laughing about me behind my back!

It was this painful thought which prevented me from barging through the cat-door of that house and going to see her. We had never gone in for meeting in her room. I did not like all the other animals in her house, and some of them were not particuarly fond of me. The one they called Bundle even curled up her nose at me and said that I "smelt". What a human, debased concept! All creatures smell. I happen to think that I smell very nice. I had assumed that my darling thought I smelt nice too. Now, I had my doubts.

All through the long dark hours of that unhappy night, I paced the gardens and walls and shed roofs of the street, thinking these sad thoughts. And by the time the church clock was striking four, I had convinced myself that I was the greatest fool on earth. Love! What was it but a human word, a human idea? I must have picked it up unconsciously somewhere, perhaps from the Sisters, or perhaps in some of the idiot talk of the other cats in the Commune. Merely because one cat found another one beautiful did not mean that they were "in love". What a ridiculous idea! We had had some fun, my beloved and I. And now she had tired of me, and she had told me so in the only manner that she could: by failing to come and meet me. What a fool I had been to think that cats could ever form a pair, and roam the world together, a sort of feline parody of Jim and June. Cats just weren't *like* that! So I told myself. No, I was alone in the world, as all cats were, and once again, I must take to the road. I must leave the little street, with its deceptively kind human beings, and its nice little bowls of food put out in the kitchen of Number Twelve, and its flower bed lavatories and its bird-tables. I must seek new worlds, new lands, and wander the earth pursuing the destiny which was prepared for me by our great Mother-of-Night.

Our great Mother was shining down on me from the cold heavens. She was alone, as I was, and She would lead me. Behind her, the sky was lightening, a pale winter grey. I would, I told myself, set out that instance. Well, perhaps not that instant. I slithered down the wall into the garden of Number Eighteen and looked up at the window of my beloved's room.

"Goodbye!" I called.

There was no answer.

Now, I would go.

But I did not go. I found that I was sitting there, and staring. This was silly. I would definitely go.

"Goodbye," I called again.

"Calling for Tammy?" said a winsome cat's voice through the darkness. I recognized it as the black and white female they call Bundle.

It was not worth a reply.

"Of course not," I replied. "Just exercising my lungs. Waiting for the birds to wake up, and then I shall be off."

"She won't come out tonight," said Bundle. "How can she?"

"Tammy?" I pretended that the word meant nothing to me. "Good Lord, no. Just off, as a matter of fact. As I said, just as soon as I've had breakfast."

"Off?"

"Yes. I've had enough of this street. I'm on my way."

Bundle clearly did not believe me.

"She's found her way into the heiring cupboard," said Bundle. "None of the people know yet. She told me to come out and tell you. She's very near her time."

"Near her time?"

"Never heard of a cat having kittens before?" asked Bundle. "You must have led a sheltered life."

And then a great joy came into my heart, and I knew why she had not been able to come out and meet me, and all my doubts and fears vanished.

"You'd better not come in and see her," said Bundle.

154

"People might see you, and then they'd follow you and disturb the kittens."

"Have they ... they been born, then?" I asked excitedly.

"None of us know. A girl likes to be on her own at a time like this," said Bundle knowingly. "But she asked me to tell you, and I have."

And she scampered back through the cat-door into the house.

CHAPTER NINETEEN

The whole of the next day and night were, for me, an agony of waiting; but of course, when I say "agony", this was a feeling quite different from the dreadful hopelessness of the previous day. In that black mood, I had doubted whether She loved me; whether She had loved me; and these doubts made the whole of life seem horrible. But now my fears were only for her safety and happiness. I did not doubt her love; merely I worried about her sufferings, and paced about, hardly able to contain my impatience. I longed to see her.

In my excitement, appetite almost entirely deserted me, but I was for some reason quite thirsty. None of my usual haunts were open when the desire for *milk* overcame me, so I was forced to play the rather mean trick which was so popular among the communards. I don't want you imitating this, because it is easy to get your paws cut if you aren't skilful, but the procedure is as follows. You approach a bottle of milk which has been left on a front door step in the early morning. When I say "approach" it, I do not mean that you creep up on it gingerly. Pounce as if it were your worst enemy, and knock it flying. If you are very lucky the birds will have already pecked off the metal top of the milk bottle; and if you are luckier still, the glass will not break. Then the milk is nicely poured out for you over the front step and all you have to do is lick it up. If, however, the glass *is* smashed, you have to be very careful not to tread in it; and not to swallow any of it – but I hardly need tell you that.

This particular morning, I had luck at Number Sixteen. That's right, the house where you live now. The sparrows had done their useful work opening the bottle, and it was easy to upset it with a flick of the paw. There was soon a delicious white cascade running down the front step, and no broken glass. It was while I was having my breakfast that a human conversation took place over my head between the woman who lives at Number Sixteen, and Sally, my darling's minder. The woman was speaking from an upstairs window to Sally who was up and dressed on the pavement. It went as follows.

"Look at what Pufftail's done!" said the woman.

"Pufftail, you greedy old man," said Sally. I believe this impertinence was actually addressed to me! But her next words were to the woman. "Tammy had her kittens last night!"

"Really? How exciting!"

"Yes. We think it's two little girls and two little boys, but it's too soon to say, and of course, we don't want to disturb her. At dinner time yesterday, apparently, she just disappeared. I was still at work, but the other girls in the house were ever so worried. They thought to themselves, it isn't like Tammy to miss her dinner – and they couldn't find her anywhere. But she was in the airing cupboard having her ... you know."

"How sweet! And is there still a chance we might have one of the kittens?"

"Oh yes. But it's better to wait a week or two before you come and see them."

"Oh yes, we wouldn't dream of disturbing them," said the upstairs lady, with her head still poking out of the window. "Just look at Pufftail drinking all our milk. Go away, Pufftail."

"He's been hanging about Tammy ever such a lot lately. I wouldn't be surprised if he wasn't, you know..."

"The father?"

"Yes."

"I don't know that's a great recommendation," remarked the upstairs lady rudely. "I hope that if that's true, the kittens won't inherit their father's fleas and his bad manners."

"Ah!" said Sally, who, I thought had a good deal more sense in her head than this upstairs person. "He's a lovely old cat – aren't you Pufftail? Funny the way he just turned up in our road, isn't it? No one knows where he came from, or who he belongs to or anything."

At this "belongs" nonsense I looked up and put on as scornful a gaze as I could manage.

"Oh well, mustn't stand here talking all morning or I'll miss the eight o'clock bus," said Sally, and she clonked off down the pavement on her high heeled paws. One day someone will explain to me why human beings wear things on their feet – and such uncomfortable-looking things at that.

I did not stay to watch the upstairs woman become a downstairs woman, mopping up the remains of my breakfast and calling down politely-expressed but unmistakable curses on my head. I had heard all I wanted to hear. The kittens had been born, and my beloved was alive! I ran down the pavement, over the wall of Number Eighteen, and in through their cat-door at the back. Sally was always the first to get up in that household. The rest of them were asleep. But that meant that they were all in their rooms with their doors shut and their eyes closed, making that noise with their noses. Where the heiring-cupboard was I could not guess. I had never before heard of cupboards especially set aside for the birth of heirs. On the whole I approved of the notion. But where was it? I had no idea. While all bedroom doors were shut, it was hard to conduct a proper search of the house, but I did my best. There were no heirs in the kitchen cupboards, just tins, as far as I could see by leaping around the room. Luckily it was not one of those households where everyone is ridiculously fond of shutting doors, and quite a number of the tin-cupboards were open. So was a cupboard under the stairs which contained an electric noise machine – silent, thank the powers, at the moment –

and quite a few old newspapers and cardboard boxes. No heirs. After some rudimentary searches on landings and in the well-room, I started to scratch the lino outside one of the bedroom doors and demand that they show me my own offspring. At first this had no effect, but at length, a bleary-eyed young woman in a nightdress appeared at the door and said "Pufftail! What are you wanting at this hour of the morning?" She groaned and looked at her bracelet-affair. "It's only seven-thirty," she added.

They are always talking in numbers, as you must have noticed. I might very well have replied "And twenty-six to you, too, Madam." But I didn't. She, less than welcoming, added, "Go away you smelly old man," and went back to bed.

But a little while later another of the women emerged from her room, and went into the bathroom to rub her teeth with a brush. You have probably noticed the terrible smell which comes from their mouths after they have done this: a sort of pepperminty gas which really hurts your nose. After she'd scrubbed her teeth, this person could be heard cooing and ah-ing into a cupboard, and I concluded that she had found the heirs. My hackles went up. I felt that she was shoving her nose in where it was not wanted; more, in some primitive way I wanted to protect the little ones, even though I knew this particular woman meant them no harm. But it was she, to give her her due, who allowed me my first glimpse of the little family. For she turned and said, "Pufftail, don't be angry. There are some little babies in the cupboard. Yes, there are. Yes, there are!" And she did something which normally I never allow a human being to do, she picked me up. In the weakness of the moment, I did not struggle. She did not exactly hold me anyway. Rather, she knelt by the door of the heiring cupboard with me on her lap and together we looked at the heirs.

My beloved was suckling them: four tiny little creatures — two young gingers, and two with tabby and white markings, similar to those of her parents. It was the very picture of contentment. It touched in me something very deep. It is hard to put into words what I felt when I looked at the scene. But it felt as if I were remembering something of my own life before memory itself had begun. I think, for a moment of peculiar and irrecoverable happiness, I was myself a newborn kitten again, in that back bedroom with my own dear mother.

There is nothing so mysterious as life itself. Where had these little beings *come* from? Only a few months before, there was no trace of their existence. Next there was a mere swelling inside their mother. And now here they were, each with full and completely independent existences, each with minds and characters of their own, each perfectly formed, each – *themselves*, when before, there was none of them. And I thought of the conversations which I had had with my beloved about the Great Stillness. I thought – as I still think – that her idea was completely crazy, that *all* things pass into this Stillness. But as I looked at her and her kittens, I had a further thought. Even if it is true that we all die, the Great Stillness itself cannot conquer *this* – this miracle of coming-into-life out of nothing! It may be that we think that the Stillness is the end of everything. But there is always this to defy it. I was not *consoled* in that moment for the killing of my brother, nor for any of the waste which goes on around us all the time. Nothing can console us for these stupid, needless killings. But the strength of the killings seemed weaker as I looked at the heirs, and heard their contented purring while their mother fed them.

She knew I was there without opening her eyes.

"Sorry I didn't come back after dinner yesterday," she murmured, "I just felt myself coming over a bit queer."

It was the usual ironical style in which we spoke to one another.

"Probably something you ate," I said.

"Probably," she smiled.

"Anyway, you seem to have made some nice friends in there," I said.

160

"Oh, they'll do," she said. "When they learn to wash. Ouch! They can bite." And she sat up for a moment, and picked one away from her breast, lifted it up in her mouth and licked it all over. "What a shock you are going to have, little sir, when you open your eyes," said She to her kitten. "The world does look a very funny place, I can tell you that much."

For a minute or two she lay back again. This time her eyes were open, and she looked straight at me.

"I've missed you," she said.

"I've missed you too," said I.

"Come and see me," she said. "Often. I can't get out at the moment, as you can see, I'm rather tied up. Ouch! All right then, if you insist, have some more milk," and she nudged the hungry little chap towards her nipple.

In the next few weeks, I saw her as often as I could; but that was not nearly often enough. Probably for the best of reasons, human beings at Number Eighteen kept the bathroom door shut for most of the time, and discouraged visitors, whether human or feline. I could not tell whether they realized my case was different, and that I was not just "any old visitor". So much of the time was spent making abortive visits to the house, and then pacing out again into the garden, having failed to see either her or the heirs.

From occasional snatches of gossip from Bundle, or between the Upstairs Woman and Sally I gathered that the kittens were growing into strong, vigorous little beings.

But there then followed a period when I neither saw them nor their mother. I suppose that by then the young ones were starting to scamper about, and it was not safe to leave the door of their room open. So Sally kept them shut up while she went off to work.

I thought a lot about them at that time, and wondered what sort of life they were all going to have. How little *I* had known at their age of what the future held in store!

Meanwhile, life in its humdrum way went on. I lurked

about the street, getting on with things, until the time came for my beloved to be separated from her children. I knew that this would be painful for her (I remembered the miaowings of my own poor mother when she was separated from her kittens!). But the whole future together lay ahead; and that was really all that mattered to me. I did not imagine a future with the kittens. No cat that I know of lives in the human way, with parents and children and grandchildren, all growing up in the same house. And to judge by how little the human beings seem to enjoy that arrangement, this is probably just as well for us. No. The kittens must grow up and lead their own lives, and I could only hope that they would escape danger and cruelty.

I had begun to think again of the time just after I escaped from the laboratory, and of that field, so full of mice and voles and other creatures. It had been, in so many ways, pleasanter than the town; and by now the corn would be growing again in the fields. We would set off in that direction when the time came. By day we would sleep together in the large old oak tree; when night came, what hunting there would be!

I felt impatient for our new life to begin; and yet, because I was so certain that it would begin quite soon, I was able to wait. Being without her reminded me of how intensely boring life could be. What was there to do, except eat, and sniff about the place, and doze, and then eat something else? Once upon a time, I had found these activities ends in themselves. But no more. Now life only seemed to be interesting if I could share it with her. And she would come.

Since I do not go in for the human habit of counting the days, I cannot tell you how long it was before she came. Sometimes I waited for her at the back door of Number Eighteen, or at our special place on the roof of the old garden shed. And sometimes I paced up and down the street at the front of her house, jumping in and out of the front gardens, and looking about for any small creatures who might lurk there. At other times, looking carefully both ways to avoid the engines of murder, I crossed the street and sat on the low wall and looked across at the door of Number Eighteen. And this was what I was doing when she took me by surprise.

It was a misty, cold night, the sort of night when the very air makes your fur moist, and breath from your mouth and nostrils appears like smoke. And there I sat on the wall opposite, looking across at her house, and not thinking about anything in particular. Suddenly, from the shadows at the side of the house, she appeared. She did not see me at first. She was looking about in an agitated manner, and stealthily, as though she was not meant to be there. She looked tired and thin, and even a little haggard. The experience of nursing the kittens was evidently exhausting her. But when she jumped up on the crumbly brick pillar by the front of her house, I saw her in all her beauty by the light of the street lamp, and she seemed lovelier than ever. Perhaps now that she had had the kittens, her beauty was less formally perfect than when I first saw her. But she was, nevertheless, more beautiful. I cannot explain it to you. There was a new dignity about her. And the white of her fur, against its tabby markings, was so very white; and her eyes were so large and intelligently green. And then those eyes, which had been looking up and down the street with such a worried expression, gazed across and caught my own, and a smile of complete radiance came over her features.

"I thought you'd gone off without me!" she called across the street.

"I thought you'd forgotten I existed!" I called back, in our old mocking tone.

"Oh, I've missed you!" she called.

"I've missed *you*!" said I.

And even as I said it, she was jumping down and bounding across the road. What happened next occurred in an instant, and yet I saw each separate part of the tragedy quite clearly as if it was being played out with excruciating slowness. I saw the headlights of the engine of murder, which seemed to come from nowhere out of the fog. I heard its murderous noise. I saw Her, with a look of heedless silly joy on her face as she ran towards me. I saw the engine of murder swerve, and heard the squeal of its brakes as it stopped. But the squeal of its brakes was deafened by another, more terrible squeal, and then there followed a yet more terrible silence. A man got out of the engine of murder. I can't remember what idiot thing he said. Something like, "Blimey, I've run over a cat!"

"It wasn't your fault," said an idiot female voice from inside the engine, and I heard the voice with the real hatred of despair, and thought, How dare you be still alive, you worthless female fool – while She, She – is lying there. The man dragged the lifeless body to the side of the road, looked up and down the street anxiously, and then drove on. While all this happened, I had retreated to the shadows, but now I came out, and looked down on what lay in the gutter. A little blood trickled from the corner of her mouth, and since that was the only sign of injury, it was impossible to believe that she was seriously hurt. By the light of the lamp, she looked so very very beautiful, lying there, but her bright green eyes now stared quite vacantly. I leant over her, and rubbed my nose against her face, but there was no response, no movement of any kind, no breath, no life. That terrible enemy which I shall never understand had taken away the creature I most loved in the world; taken her away for ever. I knew what had happened, and yet I did not know. I still allowed myself to think that it must all be some terrible game; that she would soon blink her eyes, and shake herself and laugh and we would scamper off together into the shadows. But now, the front door of Number Eighteen had opened, and there were high, sad human voices. Someone ran across the street and picked up what lay in the gutter. And I watched from the shadows as they carried her back into the house. Then I walked off slowly into the night.

CHAPTER TWENTY

I badly needed a fight, but I bided my time. Slowly and carefully I chose my path through the foggy night until this street and everyone I knew here was far away. The further north you go the houses get bigger; the steps up to the front doors are gentler; the lawns are wider. But the cats there are the same as they are everywhere; so, I dare say, are the idiot human beings.

In a wide tree-lined street in this different suburb I got the fight I was looking for. I was following up my usual practice of hugging the very inner edge of the pavement, walking along the edge of a wall built garishly of red and blue bricks. Above the wall was a privet hedge so I could not see much of the house I was passing. But when the wall and the hedge stopped I came to a large open gate and a gravel drive where a couple of engines of murder were standing. And beneath one of these engines I saw a pair of bright malicious eyes. The eyes were looking me up and down. The possessor of the eyes was in a very distinct advantage since I could not see him but he could see me in the orange glare of the street light. I advanced a pace on to the gravel.

The voice which came from beneath the car was sort of pseudo-posh. Although it was completely feline it had some of the pretentiousness which you would normally associate with our two-footed friends. There was a great deal of almost mewing and umming in his voice.

"Mm, mm, and where do you suppose you're going?"

"Are you talking to me?" I asked.

"No mm mm . . ." He was smirking at his own wit. "No hawkers, and no, mm, trespassers here. Thank you!"

A maddening titter accompanied this drollery.

"I assume you are talking to someone else, but all the same, I should like you to step out here," I said.

"Oh dear! How very mm, mm, immoderate! I fear we cannot provide what you are obviously looking for..."

"What's that?"

"My dear fellow! Isn't it mm, mm, obvious? A bath!"

And he simpered – a parody of human laughter.

If there is anything I hate in a cat it is gentility.

"All the same," I said, "I should be most grateful if you would come out from under that contraption."

"Oh you would, would you?"

"Yes."

"And might a cat ask why?"

"Yes. I want to hit your stupid head."

As I had discerned he was a fool and he came out to rise to this challenge.

"I say that's really no way to speak to another mm, mm, chap," he said, as he stalked out from beneath the exhaust pipe. But I did not give him the chance to finish the sentence. It died on his lips as I cuffed him on the side of the head so vehemently that I sent him flying.

He was a very well made white cat, almost my size. I suppose you think that I ought only to fight cats of my own size, but if I did that I should never fight anyone. Like the coward he was he jumped up quickly recovering from the blow, and ran up the front steps mewing and screaming to be let in.

"Oh no you don't," I said.

I leapt up the steps after him and jumped at his throat. He was a good fighter when I forced him to it; and, with claws outstretched, he responded to my violent embrace. Clinging to each other with fury we rolled down the steps and sent three milk bottles to smithereens in the process.

"Hawker, am I?"

"Yes."

"Trespasser, am I?"

166

"Yes, you filthy..."

"Filthy, am I?"

"Yes!"

For the moment he had the advantage. He shook himself free, punched me twice on the face and then jumped on my back. "A filthy trespassing hawker is just what you are. Filth, filth, filth!" he squealed.

"You don't speak to me like that." By now my fury was total. I was a thing possessed. This was not fighting for territory or food or love. It was fighting purely for its own sake. It was simple, naked aggression. And the fight was good and hard and long. The house was dark behind us. No one seemed anxious to rescue my enemy. No human voice intruded upon the energy of the scene and no bucket of water ended it. I began to taste his blood on my lips and to be aware that I was tearing not only his fur but his very flesh. I was pretty much the worse for wear myself for my adversary gave very nearly as good as he got. But I was too big and strong for him. I could have killed him but I did not want to. As suddenly as the fight began, it ended. We had both had enough and he limped off to a flower bed and climbed a tree. It was a soft-barked cedar: about the easiest tree in the world to climb. I could have followed him but I could not be bothered. I did not even bother to snarl back when he called down from the branches over my head, "If you want to know what I think of you, I think you're mm, mm, a howling cad!"

I was not listening. In the next garden I had heard something that interested me and my ears had not played me false. It was the voice of a pretty little black piece.

"Oh, you were brave!"

And when I got closer, "Oh! You are wounded. Let me lick you better. Is that better? Is it, old hero?" And it was.

She kept me happy for half an hour, and then I limped off again to another garden and further adventures. Because it was so perishing cold there was not much in the way of game, and what there was had been scooped up by the

167

wretched owls. But I managed to find a sort of hutch affair at the bottom of one of the gardens, where the door was loose on its latch; so that night I was rewarded with a rabbit supper.

I suppose you think I was callous. This was the night when I had lost someone who was – well, as I've said – pretty special to me. And I spent it fighting and wenching and hunting. I dare say it was callous. I am simply telling you what I did. Nor, strangely, did I feel *anything* for a couple of days: feel anything about Her accident, that is to say. There was such absence of feeling that I began to think that I had dreamed the whole extraordinary story of our love. I just was not that sort of cat. I had been living a sort of fantasy. I did not actually *care* that she was dead at all.

Besides, I had come to a really posh neighbourhood where the pickings and takings were wonderful. The two-footed family who had been fattening up the rabbit for me had also been keeping a couple of guinea-pigs as an entrée and very succulent they were. There were dustbins and larders a-plenty. And the female population kept one consoled. Thus I lived for three or four days and nights. And then, exhausted, I found myself somewhere to sleep in a broken-down wicker chair at the corner of someone's shed and slept there among the cobwebs for many an hour. And it was when I woke from that sleep that my haunting sense of loss began. You know the way that when you wake from a really deep sleep you do not know quite where you are and all the memory gets fuddled and strange? I thought that I was waking up in "our" garden shed; and my first thought on waking was that I must jump over the fence and see Her. I had even forgotten about the kittens. In that waking moment I was still stuck in the early days of our love; the happiest time, as I now think, of my whole life. And then, with hideous clarity, as I stood up, I remembered everything. I could not go next door to see Her because I was a mile away from her house and She was no longer there. The accident, and the sight of her beautiful staring features by the kerb-stone, all came back to me. The memory of them was a torture. And I knew that life could never really be happy again.

The desire just to see Her drove me wild. I knew that I couldn't. I knew that the horrible Stillness had fallen upon her and Sally or the others would have got rid of the body somehow or another. I knew all that. But still, uppermost in my heart was the desire to see Her, to talk to her, to feel her close to me. Very faint in the afternoon sky, our Great Mother could just be seen, a little white disc against the pale grey.

"If I could see her once," I prayed. "Just once." But I knew that it was an absurd desire which could never ever be granted. She was too good for this silly, filthy, two-footed world. But that was the place where I must drag out my pointless existence; pointless and miserable, without her.

I could not be still once the memory of Her had returned. I was unable to sit or stand for a single moment. I paced the shed. Then I went out and paced the frosty lawn. I climbed a fence and then I jumped down again. I slithered under a hedge and back. It felt as though I could not stop this idiot, manic activity. I started to eat less and all the chasing and pacing about exhausted me so that I had long unhappy patches of sleep at extraordinary times, like in the middle of the night, when I would normally never dream of sleeping. There was no remedy. And as far as I could see there was no likelihood of the painful memory ever getting better. Oh, I was a fool to think that I had been unhappy before I met Her! True, there had been unhappy moments and long spells of very great pain and fear and distress. But these bad moments had all been isolated ones. When the pain or the fear stopped, existence continued its colourless round. It was just going on in the background. I did not *notice* every passing minute. Nearly all the time just evaporated as I slouched about eating and biffing and chasing the females. At the time, I could not possibly have guessed that this – time passing without your noticing it – is the greatest possible blessing. For now, in this new phase of life, I found that

I noticed every second which passed. And time itself seemed to be torturing me by passing so slowly. And there was nothing worth living for.

I tried to be cynical. (Here was a turn-up for the books! Trying to be cynical! Normally it was my nature to be so.) I tried to tell myself that I had arrived in a very posh neighbourhood where the pickings were good and you could get your kip undisturbed. Since life was now a pointless extension of conscious misery the least I could do was to make myself comfortable, to eat well, to sleep well and to enjoy what diversions the kitchens and gardens of this posh suburb had to offer. And perhaps if I had not felt so tired and so funny about food this scheme might have worked. It might have worked if I was not so uncommonly agitated, pacing about, as the two-footers say, like a cat on hot bricks. Horrible expression that Jim Harbottle was very fond of using.

The trouble was I was not in the mood to enjoy anything. And although I tried to make some sort of life for myself in that suburb, it was no use. I knew that I wanted to get back to my old haunts where I had known happiness with Her. I even had this stupid thought that if I got back to the spot where the accident happened, I might find that it had been all some kind of mistake; that she was really alive and waiting for me... I knew this was nonsense, I knew it would never happen and yet to all my other sorrows there was the added sorrow of false hope that it might be true. That was the sort of state I was in.

Thus it was, very gradually, that I set off in the direction of this street. Or so I imagined. I crossed road after road. The houses became more Harbottlian. And then they stopped altogether and I came to a vast ring of road where the engines of murder came at one another from all sides and drove round and round in circles. Some sort of game, I suppose. Horrible great thing. So I realized that I was lost and that I would never find my way back and this did not cheer me up very much as you can imagine. But I did retrace my steps into the town. There was not anything *else* worth doing so I paced and paced along being a good deal more cautious even than usual about crossing the roads. As a matter of fact there were hardly any engines of murder about. The nearer the centre of the town I got, the quieter things became. Only in the middle of the town was there much sign of life. A group of some dozen two-footers, all dressed in the same sort of manner, were standing in the main square. The males had peaked caps and the females wore extraordinary bonnets with curly bits at the side. They all held huge lumps of metal to their lips but the sound they made was euphonious. At their side there was a large fir tree. One of the strangest trees you ever saw in your life. It was actually growing electric light bulbs and they were all alight. I know that you will think I had been walking too far and that the tiredness had gone to my head. You will be thinking that I dreamt it. But I swear to you it was an electric light bulb tree.

A small gaggle of two-footers were standing around the light bulb tree and listening to the uniform people make the music with the metal in their mouths. And I approached, because this was interesting, and because there was nothing better to do. You can imagine my surprise when I heard my "name" coming into some of the two-footing conversation!

A woman was standing there with two younger females, little more than children. "I love Christmas carols," said the woman. "And I love the dear old Sally Army band." This was an amazing revelation. I had never been too sure what armies were, but I gathered that they were large groups of two-footers, not unlike a commune, which ganged together for the purposes of fighting. My darling's minder, Sally, appeared to have one of these armies all of her own.

"I think this is going to be the nicest Christmas ever," said one of the girls, "now that we've got a kitten."

"I think so too," said the woman.

"Look," said the girl who had not yet spoken. "That's Pufftail!"

171

"Oh, shut up," said the other girl. "You're always saying things like that."

"Look for yourself."

"All cats look like that," said the other girl, rather absurdly. "Quite a lot do anyway."

"Not as large as that," said her sister, "and not with such a big fluffy tail, and not with that frightening angry expression on their faces, and not with half an ear missing."

"I really think it might be Pufftail," said the woman. "But don't touch him if it *is*. I don't want our lovely little kitten catching fleas."

This was Upstairs Woman who spoke through the window to Sally. And from their extremely insulting remarks I deduced that they had recognized me. One of the children approached me and looked horribly as if she were going to try to stroke me. I hissed and raised my hackles as fiercely as I could.

"You see," said the other, more prudent child, "that's Pufftail."

After they had heard the metal-blowing for a few more minutes, the little family agreed they were cold.

"And have we bought all our presents?" asked Upstairs Woman.

"It's too late now," said one of the children. "It's Christmas Eve and all the shops are shutting. Isn't it exciting? It's Christmas Eve!"

"And we have a kitten for Christmas."

"But don't tell Daddy," said Upstairs Woman. "It's his surprise."

It was a relief to hear that they had finished their shopping. If I kept my distance I could follow them home and revisit all my sad haunts. It would be torture to do so but worse torture to stay away. And so I followed the trio who were carrying bags of parcels and baskets of holly and mistletoe. And the walk from the electric light bulb tree to their street was a surprisingly short one.

172

"Can you see who's following us?" said one of the children.

"The one you call Pufftail," said the other.

"Don't talk too loud," said the woman. "Just let's ignore him and pretend we haven't seen him."

"Dirty old thing," said one of the children.

"That's not very nice," said the other girl. "He's no dirtier than we would be if we lived out in the streets all the time."

"Thank you, Madam," I said, but she took no notice.

"How would you like it if your wife had been run over," she went on.

"I couldn't have a wife, could I?" said the sister.

"You know what I mean."

I am not sure that I did, but the child went on, "I think he's come back to see his kittens."

"They don't know that sort of thing," said Upstairs Woman. "I think he's just come back on the scrounge. Well, I'm not giving him anything because we really don't want such a dirty old thing in the house."

"They let him into the kitchen at Number Twelve."

"That's their affair."

"Well, I think he should be allowed to see Tabitha. She is his own daughter."

"We don't know that," said Upstairs Woman.

So they went indoors and slammed the door in my face.

I wandered up and down the back gardens disconsolately. Perhaps it had been a mistake to come back. And yet there was something almost consoling about my return and about seeing all the places and sheds and walls and fences which We had made our own.

I was anxious to know what had happened to the kittens. One of them had gone to Number Sixteen. But what of the others? There was a very nasty moment when I bumped into Rocket, the ginger tom from next door, who informed me that all the kittens had been drowned. But this turned out to be a false rumour. "More's the pity," said Bundle. "They've decided to keep all three, but they've given one to the people at Number Sixteen. A Christmas present, they say, whatever Christmas is."

"It's to do with lights and trees," I said. Bundle let me in for a snoop round at Number Eighteen and then I went up the road to Number Twelve where they fed me very handsomely — some sort of fowl I think — and let me sleep on a cushion in the corner of the kitchen.

I slept very long and very deep and when I woke in the night I decided not to go out but simply to lie there and enjoy the feeling that I was back among friends. I dozed and I sat and I sat and dozed. And by the time I had finished dozing, the morning light had appeared.

"Good morning, Pufftail," said the two-footer who inhabited Number Twelve. "A very merry Christmas," and she put down in front of me a plate of uncommonly palatable liver.

When I had finished it, I went a few doors down to Number Sixteen. Already the whole family were up and the place was a riot of paper and silly hats and quarrels. I noticed they had a tree — a much smaller tree than the magic one and with no electric lights but the same shape. I sat on the window-sill and looked at the tree and for a moment I thought that my wildest hopes and dreams had come true. On the branches of the tree there were coloured balls made of glittery stuff. The sort of thing that any cat would want to smash if he or she was able. And there was a little cat who was doing excellent work with the glittery globes, jumping up at them and biffing them and biting them as if they were young blackbirds. And it was, but was not, Her! The resemblance to my beloved was uncanny. The same white chest, the same ribbed tail, and, when she turned, the same delicate face, white around the mouth and a yellowish tabby around the brow and nose. And, yes! The same extraordinary bright green eyes.

Well, you have guessed. This was the cat they had decided

174

to call Tabitha. And she is your mother, young kitten; and perhaps you can guess now why I am rather fond of her and rather fond of you...

Pufftail paused, the fluffy old street cat, and looked down into his grandson's eyes.

"I think," said he, "that I have probably told you enough about my life for now. Of course, I shan't stay long in this neighbourhood. Once I had seen your mother settled, I waited to see her have kittens of her own. And now I have seen you settled, I shall have had enough of settling. It won't be long now before I take to the road once more and stroll away and forget all about you. And you will forget all about me. But try to remember some of the things I have told you. Remember never to trust a two-footed thing. Remember..." But even as he spoke, Tabitha, light of foot and bright of eye, came towards them over the lawn.

"Still talking!" she laughed.

"Grandpapa was telling me that he was going to go off on his travels again," said the young kitten. "Can I go with him? Please, Mother."

"And where is it this time?" asked Tabitha. "The car park? The next street? The roundabout? Yes, he has the most exciting travels, don't you, old man?" Pufftail was about to splutter. But she continued, "I expect you are hungry. What can I get you? A chicken leg? One has been injudiciously left on the larder shelf."

And with rather a satirical twitch of her tail, Tabitha trotted back into the house to fetch her father something to eat.

THROUGH THE DOLLS' HOUSE DOOR

Jane Gardam

Claire and Mary love the dolls' house and its curious assortment of residents: the outsize Dutch doll, Miss Bossy; the General and his troop of Trojan soldiers; the miserable Small Cry; the mysterious Sigger... But little do the girls know of the extraordinary lives and adventures, past and present, of this resourceful band and the marvellous stories they have to tell.

"An original story... wry and funny, and full of sharply poignant sense of the passage of time."
Jill Paton Walsh, *Books For Keeps*